Joey was watching the man's mouth, waiting for him to say something, when she saw small but very long, dark fingers reach up and curl into his hand.

The man stepped aside. At the height of his knee, a big-eared, amber-eyed face peeked around at her from behind his legs.

Joey gasped. "A monkey."

The old man shook his head, then made the letter "N" with his right hand and snapped it sharply. NO. NO. "She's a chimpanzee."

For a second, Joey thought the chimp was clutching a stuffed toy, but when it opened its hand a gray kitten scampered away and jumped off the deck. The chimp brought two fingers to its eyes, then stretched the V toward Joey.

"She is saying 'I see you,'" the old man said, and made the same sign.

I-SEE-YOU, Joey signed back, then grinned.

Hurt
Go
Happy

Ginny Rorby

A Tom Doherty Associates Book
New York

This is a work of fiction. All of the characters, organizations, and events portrayed in this book are either products of the author's imagination or are used fictitiously.

HURT GO HAPPY

A Starscape Book
Published by Tom Doherty Associates, LLC
175 Fifth Avenue
New York, NY 10010

www.tor-forge.com

ISBN-13: 978-0-7653-5304-7
ISBN-10: 0-7653-5304-0

First Edition: August 2006
First Mass Market Edition: January 2007

Printed in the United States of America

0 9 8 7 6 5 4 3 2

To Belinda, John Hopkins, Lucy,

and a dead dog

The American Sign Language Alphabet

a

b

c

d

i

j

k

l

m

r

s

t

u

0

1

2

3

4

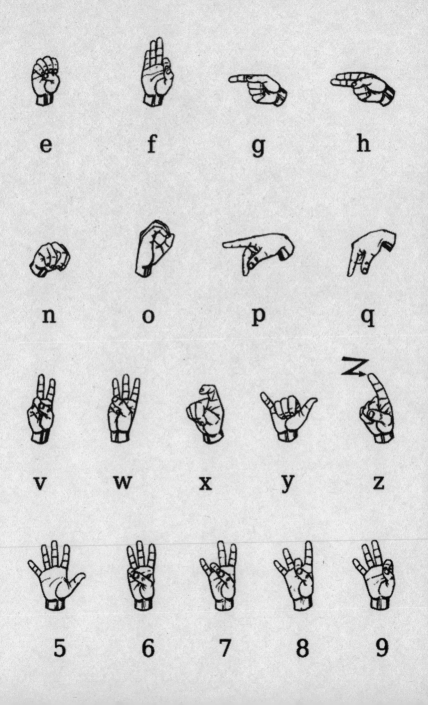

e   f   g   h

n   o   p   q

v   w   x   y   z

5   6   7   8   9

Chapter One

February 1991
Fort Bragg, California

The vibration of someone moving through the house woke Joey. She opened her eyes with a start, her heart racing. The room was pitch black, but it was getting light outside. She could see the dim outline of the deck beyond her sliding glass doors and the redwood tree that grew beside it. *It's just Ray.* Her heart slowed.

The blank face of her digital clock showed that the electricity was still out from the storm of five days before. Even Joey, who was *nearly* as deaf as a post, had heard the explosion of the transformer on the pole in the yard that made her mother flinch and her brother clap his hands over his ears a moment before the lights went out.

They weren't alone; the winds had gusted to eighty-five miles an hour, knocking the power out along the entire coast, and they were sealed off. A mudslide to the north had covered the route to Leggett, and the Navarro River was out of its banks and over the south road to Cloverdale. Downed trees blocked the other three coast-to-inland roads. Only someone like her stepfather Ray, with a knowledge of the web of logging roads that lay across the mountains, could have gotten in or out.

With the pattern of getting up for school broken, Joey couldn't remember what day it was. *Wednesday,* she thought. *No. It's Thursday.* Last night they'd gone to Fort Bragg for their first good meal in days. All the meat in Safeway's freezer had defrosted, but instead of pitching it, the employees barbecued every scrap and invited the town. She still felt full, smiled, and wondered vaguely why Ray was up so early—a logging-truck driver with no logs to haul—before she rolled over and went back to sleep.

When she woke again it was light. She turned to look out the sliding glass doors beside her bed and brought her hand from beneath the covers to brush her hair from her eyes. Her left thumb was damp and wrinkled. It had been so long since she'd awakened to find her thumb wet that she'd lulled herself into thinking she'd finally outgrown sucking it. She grabbed it with her right hand and squeezed it over and over like a sponge.

For the first time in five days, sunlight slanted through the trees along the trail behind the house, though raindrops still clung to the redwood leaves, sparkling like Christmas lights. She lay and watched them, waiting for the wrinkles in her thumb to disappear so her mother wouldn't know she had started again. She tried to remember what she'd dreamed that had made her anxious. That's what the county psychologist had told her to do. Face her fears. Don't let them burrow in.

A breeze brushed the redwood leaves but the raindrops held on. She imagined herself as small as a drop of water falling from the sky, thinking herself a goner only to be saved at the last moment by a spiky green finger. She stared at one drop in particular, as if guarding it, until a rougher breeze knocked it loose to shatter on the deck.

Joey examined her thumb. It was nearly back to normal. *Why do I do this?* she wondered again. *I'm safe—in my own room.* Her own room. Since his birth, she'd shared the front bedroom with Luke. Then, four months ago, the builders had finished the second-story addition and Ray and her mother moved upstairs. Their old room, with its view of the creek and the forested canyon, became hers.

Before she'd lost her hearing, she'd loved the whisper of wind through pines, and since she had no way of knowing how different it sounded in a redwood forest, the sight of branches swaying re-created that sound in her mind. Even after six and a half years of deafness, she sometimes awoke expecting her hearing to have returned, like her sight, with the dawn.

Joey wasn't totally deaf. The doctors had told her mother that she'd lost about 70 percent of her hearing, leaving her able to hear lawn mowers, chainsaws, horns honking, sirens, her brother's wails when he was hungry and his shrieks when he was hurt. All other sounds were lost. Still, over the years, she'd gotten used to the silence, and liked it in many ways. She did miss the quiet rhythm of normal conversation, birds singing, and music. Listening with her eyes always reminded her of Smiley, the nickname she'd given her nurse in the hospital because of the yellow smiley-face button she wore. On the day

Joey's mother told her she was deaf, Smiley had made it seem like a gift, promising Joey that she would always keep the memory of certain sounds—phantoms, she called them—like her mother's voice, rain, and the wind through pines. Smiley said she could attach those remembered sounds to whatever she pleased, even to silent things like leaves falling and butterflies.

She lay for a while with her thumb jammed into her fist and watched the music of the tree limbs swaying until she was jolted by the slamming of the door to the bedroom she used to share with her brother. The house would soon shudder and tremble with the energy of a two-and-a-half-year-old.

Joey stretched and yawned, pulled the covers to her chin, and hugged herself. The air in her room was frigid because she never used the heater, even when the power was on. She hated the feel and smell of electric heat. She preferred socks, long-johns, and piles of warm blankets no matter how cold it got. Unheated air helped her fight down the memory of rusting, over-heated trailers or bare-bones apartments sweltering in the middle of winter.

Though she liked to sleep in a cold room, she didn't like getting up in one. She scooted out of bed, jerked the spread up to cover the pillows, then darted into the woodstove-warmed hall with her shoulders hunched and her hands clamped in her armpits. She glanced down to see if the light was on in the bathroom, then remembered the power was out and opened the door slowly, in case someone was there. A candle burned in the wall-mounted candleholder her mother had bought the last time the power went out.

"Hi," she said, when she came into the kitchen from brushing her teeth with bottled water.

Her mother turned from the little two-burner Coleman stove and smiled.

"Where's Luke?" Joey asked, then watched her lips.

"Outside peeing on the roses."

"How come?"

"Ray told him it keeps the deer from eating the garden. As soon as you went into the bathroom, he grabbed his crotch and ran outside."

Joey laughed. "Is that true about the deer?"

Her mother shrugged. "Who knows?"

"Is the power still out in town?"

Ruth nodded. "Except what's on the mill's circuit, the hospital, and the harbor."

"Where'd Ray go?"

"Up there somewhere," her mother said, pointing with the spatula in the direction of the hill behind their house, "splitting firewood. Pancakes?"

"Yes, please." Joey caught Luke's arm as he came in and kissed the top of his curly blond head.

"Ick," he shouted, giggling and squirming to free himself.

"But I love kissing you," Joey crooned and swung him off the ground to smooch the back of his neck.

When she put him down he whirled and stomped his foot. "No kisses," he hollered.

Joey pretended to get the urge again and chased him a few times around the sofa.

Her mother waved to catch her attention. "Will you get ----
------ outside to ---------- toilet with?" her mother asked, but
mid-sentence she had looked down to check the underside of
the pancake she was cooking.

"What?" Joey said.

Ruth faced her. "Sorry. Will you get a bucket of water from
the barrel outside to flush the toilet with? And finish helping
Luke dress, okay?"

"Are you going somewhere?" Joey asked.

"I told you. The radio said the power's on in the harbor. I'm
going to work." She flipped the pancake. "Could get busy."

Her mother had been a waitress at the Old Dock Café in
Noyo Harbor for nearly six years. In spite of having met Ray
during her second week on the job and marrying him six months
later, she wouldn't quit. Joey's stepfather drove a logging truck
for Georgia-Pacific, which had a big mill in town. It was a pretty
good job, though there was always the threat that he'd get in-
jured again or laid off. Her mother used that as an excuse to
keep working, but Joey knew it was because having a job, any
job, was her mother's safety net. She would never risk another
four months like their first four months in Fort Bragg.

When they arrived from Reno six and a half years ago, the job
she'd been promised was gone. The money they'd saved, hidden
in the belly of Joey's teddy bear, bought them a month in a cheap
motel on a back street in the center of town. It ran out three
months before the owner of the Old Dock Café took pity and
gave her a job. For that length of time, they had lived in their car,
eaten one meal a day of handouts from local restaurants, and depended, for their safety, on the community of other homeless

people. Her mother had sworn then that nothing short of losing both legs would get her to quit the job that had seemed like a miracle then.

Eating meals cooked on a Coleman stove reminded Joey of those days, but she smiled when her mother slid a huge pancake onto a plate and handed it to her. Joey got a knife and fork out of the drawer and the carton of milk from the ice chest in the middle of the kitchen floor. What was left of the perishables from the refrigerator were on ice in the cooler.

Her mother waved again for her attention. "Pretty day," she said. "What are your plans?"

Joey shrugged. "I don't have any. Want me to watch Luke?"

"I don't think so," her mother said.

Joey didn't bother to watch her answer. She knew what her mother would say. She'd never let her babysit. Not for a quick run to the store, not even last winter when paramedics took her to the hospital for stitches after she missed the kindling she was splitting and drove the ax through her shoe. She'd called a neighbor to watch him then had waited, bleeding and in pain, for the ten minutes it took the woman to get there before dialing 911.

It seemed to Joey that her mother treated her as if she'd stopped aging when she stopped hearing. "Do you think I might lose him or something?"

"I don't want to talk about it. You know why."

"Yeah. Right." *Too young, instead of the truth—too deaf.* Joey accepted a second pancake. "Maybe I'll ride my bike to the beach." Knowing what her mother would say to that idea, she drew a happy face on the pancake with syrup to miss her objections, but looked up too soon and saw, "---------- sea is too rough."

The rough sea was why she wanted to go. She'd never heard the sound of the ocean and she thought it might be loud enough today.

Ruth tapped her shoulder. "Did you hear me? I said I'd rather you not ride your bike today. There may still be lines down and the sea is too rough."

"Mom, I'm thirteen and a half. I won't cross a downed line and I won't go too near the water."

"No bike. No beach," her mother said. "How about looking for mushrooms for me?"

Joey gave up with a shrug. "To eat or for dye?"

Her mother boiled certain mushrooms to make a dye for wool with which she knitted sweaters, caps, and scarves.

"Both would be nice. There should be pine spikes on the hill and oyster mushrooms on that old alder by the creek."

Joey only nodded. Her mother had taken a mushroom-identification class at the college two years before. The two of them had gone hunting after every rain that winter until she had taught Joey nearly everything she'd learned. They'd even made money selling oyster mushrooms and chanterelles, enough to buy Joey a used bike, which, to this point, she'd been allowed to ride only on the logging trails in the state forest across the road from their house.

While her mother dressed for work, Joey gave some thought to ignoring her this time and riding to the beach anyway, but after Ruth left, she chickened out. Even if nothing happened, she wasn't good at deceiving her mother. The link between them had grown intuitive. If she went, Ruth would know.

Joey did the breakfast dishes with rainwater from the barrel outside the kitchen door, then added an old sweater of Ray's over her sweatshirt and a waterproof jacket from the drying hook near the woodstove. She found a trowel and a big basket in the storeroom, and from the pantry she got a stack of wax paper sandwich bags to keep the dye mushrooms, which could make you sick, separate from the mushrooms they would eat.

Just outside the front door, Joey slipped into Ray's rubber boots, then headed across the yard and down the hill to the creek. A chain girdled the bent trunk of an old tan oak tree. In summer, a rope chair-swing hung there. This was a favorite spot of Joey's. She would sit for hours and watch the birds flitting through the woods and listen with her eyes to the little waterfall. If she took a book, she could completely lose herself in its pages, then look at the waterfall and the leaves trembling in a breeze and fill her sight with sound. She loved that about being deaf; Smiley had been right, that was its gift.

Joey stopped beneath the tan oak to watch the silty, butterscotch-pudding-colored water tumble over the rocks as if it were on the boil. The creek was still high from the storm, too swollen to cross. She walked the high bank instead, scanning the thick brush for chanterelles, her personal favorite.

Joey found the alder but someone had gotten there before her. Only a few very small oyster mushrooms were left, and they were turning brown and beginning to melt. This was the thing Joey didn't like about mushrooms. They didn't die like anything else. They filled with maggots while they still looked fresh, then darkened and liquefied like something from an old horror movie, finally leaving a black tarry spot.

A yard past the alder she spotted a Pacific giant salamander as long as her foot, eating a bright yellow banana slug. She squatted down to watch, imagining first what it would be like to be the slug sliding into darkness, then she nearly made herself sick by considering the role of the salamander. She got up and stepped over them.

The storm had blown several trees down across the trail along the creek and it had become overgrown since the beginning of the rainy season in November. She climbed over and under, searching the duff cautiously for lumps that hinted at a fresh, new mushroom coming up.

Ray loved beefsteak mushrooms, not because they tasted very good but because they cooked up to look exactly like bloody, raw, well-marbled beef. He and Luke liked to act pukey, letting strips of the bloody red fungus dangle from their forks, smacking their lips. When Joey found a beautiful fresh one at the base of a fir, she thought it would be her prize of the day, but later she found herself on an unfamiliar section of the trail, farther than she had wandered before. There, spanning the creek, was another downed alder covered with satiny white oyster mushrooms.

Joey took a wax-paper bag and left her basket on the redwood duff. She climbed down the slight incline past the broken base of the alder and collected the largest of the mushrooms. When that bag was full, she got another and waded nearly midstream to reach the ones along the center of the log.

It was when she turned back with the second bag full that she saw the old man. She froze, her heart pounding. He had her basket and he was very mad.

Joey gulped to keep a scream from escaping. Angry faces terrified her and his was red to the point of bursting. He was yelling at her, making it hard to read the furious flurry of words. He reached in the basket, grabbed the beefsteak mushroom, and shook it at her. "Thief," he said. She caught that word because the tongue whips out like a snake's with words that begin with "th."

Instinctively, she took a step backward. The creek flowed over the rim of her boot and filled it with icy water. She was trapped now, unable to run if she had to.

He must have seen that he was scaring her, because he calmed down a little and put the beefsteak mushroom back in the basket. "You're trespassing," he said, shaking a gnarly finger at her. "I'm sick ---------- people ---------- mushrooms."

"What did you say?" she stammered, though it was clear enough since he'd called her a thief. People were very territorial about the mushrooms on their property.

He said something else and pointed up the hill. Joey's eyes followed the jab of his finger and for the first time she saw the small dark house nearly hidden by the trees. His head jerked and he blinked as if he'd been slapped. "Oh my," he said. DEAF YOU? He brought his index finger to his right ear then brought his hands together like elevator doors closing then pointed at her.

Joey remembered that sign. It was one Smiley had taught her before she left the hospital. One secret she had successfully kept from her mother, who didn't want her to learn to sign, was that she still practiced the alphabet with the old *Sesame Street* sign language book that Smiley gave her the day after the doctors said her hearing loss was permanent.

She nodded. Her foot was very cold. She slipped it out of the boot, which was so heavy with water it was hard to lift. Keeping an eye on the old man, she emptied it, then waded slowly toward shore. She froze when he stepped toward her.

He brought his fist to his chest and made a circle with it. "I'm sorry," he said, and held out his hand.

She put the bag of mushrooms in it.

He turned and put them in her basket. "You can have them," he said slowly, pronouncing each word carefully. "I don't know one mushroom from another."

The cold water was making Joey's foot ache. She stepped up on the bank a few feet away, still watching him cautiously, though now that he was calm, she could see that this small, white-haired, brittle-looking man was too old to be afraid of.

She'd missed some of what he'd said about the mushrooms, but now he was asking her something that ended in "---------- sign language."

By catching the last two words, she guessed he was asking her if she used it. People who did not depend on reading lips didn't realize how many words create the same mouth shape. He had probably said "do you use . . ."—three words that only pucker the lips.

"No," she said.

He shook his head, sadly, then patted his pockets, looking for something he wasn't able to find. "Can you read my lips?"

"Some."

"Come with me," he said, and pointed up the steep hill.

She didn't move.

"It's okay," he said, signing, OKAY.

Still she didn't move. "I don't think I'd better." She saw by a little facial flinch that he understood very well that he'd scared her.

"Wait here then," he said, using a "stay" hand signal as if she were a dog. "Until I get a pencil and paper."

She nodded.

Joey watched the old man climb up through the trees. He did so slowly, resting often with one hand against a tree trunk and the other at his chest. When he was still yards from the top, he stopped again, looked back, and tried to smile. His face was red and his chest heaved.

Joey watched him stand there for a full minute trying to catch his breath and staring up at the house, still a hundred feet away. He started to climb again, but had taken only a few steps when his left foot went out from under him. He fell heavily and began to slide down the trail. Joey grabbed her basket, jammed her foot into the wet, cold boot, and climbed the hill to help him.

He'd caught hold of a redwood sapling, so he'd slipped only a few feet back down the hill. Joey helped him get his footing and let him lean on her until they reached the steps leading up to his back deck. That was when she saw the jungle gym in one corner, a tipped-over tricycle, and a litter of toys. Though she was no longer afraid of him, it made her more comfortable to know he was someone's grandfather.

"I'm an old goat," he said slowly, emphasizing each word, "but clearly not a mountain goat." He smiled, patted her hand,

and indicated that she should sit and wait for him. When the sliding glass doors opened again, he stepped out onto his deck with a pad of paper, then turned and motioned to someone inside.

Joey was watching his mouth, waiting for him to say something, when she saw small but very long, dark fingers reach up and curl into his hand.

The man stepped aside. At the height of his knee, a big-eared, amber-eyed face peeked around at her from behind his legs.

Joey gasped. "A monkey."

The old man shook his head, then made the letter "N" with his right hand and snapped it sharply. NO. NO. "She's a chimpanzee."

For a second, Joey thought the chimp was clutching a stuffed toy, but when it opened its hand a gray kitten scampered away and jumped off the deck. The chimp brought two fingers to its eyes, then stretched the V toward Joey.

"She is saying, 'I see you,'" the old man said, and made the same sign.

I-SEE-YOU, Joey signed back, then grinned.

"Don't show your teeth," the old man said, covering his mouth.

The little chimpanzee was wearing a diaper and a T-shirt from their local lighthouse, Point Cabrillo. "My brother wears that same outfit day and night," Joey said and laughed, then clamped a hand over her mouth.

The chimp began to sway back and forth, then ran toward her on bowed legs and knuckles. Joey held still like her mother had told her to do when a dog runs up to sniff you. But the little chimp veered off and grabbed the basket Joey had left on the top step. She dumped all the mushrooms out, put the basket over her head, and began to spin until she got dizzy and fell down.

Joey giggled.

The chimp peeked from beneath its wicker bonnet, grinned, and signed, I-SEE-YOU, again.

"I-SEE-YOU, too. May I pet her?" she asked the old man.

He nodded, then wrote on the pad and showed it to her: *But let her come to you.*

Joey sat down on the deck and crossed her ankles.

The chimpanzee rolled over and stood up. Her eyes locked on Joey's face, not boldly, but not shyly, either. Joey knew she was being judged. She knew this because it was how she herself judged the intentions of strangers.

The old man held the pad down for her to see. He'd written, *Friend.*

When Joey looked up, he signed, FRIEND, by hooking his index fingers first one way, then the other.

Joey pointed to herself, then hooked her index fingers.

The chimpanzee mimicked the sign, then glanced up at the old man, who nodded. "A new friend," he said.

She came toward Joey with one hand extended, bent at the wrist. Joey touched the back of her own wrist to the chimp's, then patted her own thigh. The chimp glanced up at the old man, who flipped his hands for her to go ahead.

The chimp turned a couple of circles, then stepped across Joey's legs and sat down. She linked her arms around Joey's neck and put her forehead against Joey's.

"Wow," Joey said. "What a wonderful girl you are." She stroked the coarse, thin hair on the chimp's head and watched her staring at her own index fingers at work in her lap, signing, FRIEND, to herself. When she lifted her head, her eyes sparkled and her lips were puckered. She kissed Joey's left eye, then pulled her head to one side and began to pick through her bushy, auburn hair.

The old man held the pad out. *She's grooming you. Her name is S-U-K-A-R-I.* He'd added the phonetic spelling: *Sue-car-e.*

No one had ever thought to do that for her. "Sukari," Joey said.

The old man nodded and smiled, then fingerspelled her name. *It's Swahili for sugar,* he wrote on the pad. *A nickname for sugar-butt.*

As if she understood, Sukari turned, put her head against Joey's knees, and pulled her diaper down so Joey could admire the fine white hairs on her bottom.

Joey put her head back and laughed out loud.

Chapter Two

Joey sat on the top step with her back against the side of the house and the baby chimpanzee balanced on her knee. She knew it was unnecessary, but she kept the fingers of her right hand spread across Sukari's narrow shoulders, as if she needed support like Luke had when he was a tippy baby. In truth, Joey wanted the energetic feel of Sukari against her palm to last forever.

Though where she sat was damp, shady, and cold, Joey felt as if her insides were roasting. How could she have imagined her day would take this turn? That she would be sitting here with a chimpanzee rifling her pockets, splaying her lips to look at her teeth, and rooting into her boots as far down as she could reach.

Joey laughed until her sides hurt. But deep inside was a truer joy, exactly like she'd felt when her mother came home from the hospital with Luke—instantaneous, heart-pounding love.

Sukari went back to sorting through sections of Joey's thick, unruly hair. When she found a spiky redwood leaf, she yanked it from the tangle.

"Ouch." Joey flinched. "That hurt."

Sukari made a loose little fist, circled her heart, then slapped the leaf back in place and covered it with a clump of hair.

The old man, who sat at the base of the jungle-gym slide, flapped his hand for Joey's attention, made the same sign, and pointed to Sukari. "She said she was sorry."

"How did she know what I said?"

He thought a moment, then wrote, *Do you have any pets?*

Joey shook her head.

How old is your brother?

"Two and a half."

"Sukari's probably three and a half," he said, then took a moment to write his answer to her question. *Even though babies can't understand what we say, they figure out what we mean from our facial expressions and the words we repeat over and over. It's how children learn language. It's the same with our pets. They don't have to understand every word to get what we mean. We say, 'Are you ready to eat dinner? Do you want to go for a walk?' and they probably hear blah, blah, blah, eat, blah, blah, blah, walk.*

Joey laughed. "That's just what I do. Catch a word or two and figure the rest out."

He clapped his hands together. "Exactly."

"Did you teach her sign language?" Joey asked.

He nodded.

"How many words does she know?"

"Twenty-five or thirty."

"Where did you get her?"

"Africa." He flicked his index finger away from his forehead. "Understand?"

"Africa, yes. Understand, yes, but what does this mean?" Joey flicked her finger off her forehead.

That's the sign for "Do you understand?"

UNDERSTAND, Sukari signed.

"Yes, I understand," Joey said and poked Sukari in the ribs.

Sukari leaned back along the length of Joey's outstretched legs until she was looking at him upside down. She brought her arms over her head and signed something.

The old man repeated the signs for Joey, then wrote, *"Tickle me, turtle." She calls me turtle because I'm slow.*

"How did she think of that?"

He held the pad so she could see his answer: *In addition to Hidey, the kitten, she has a pet tortoise.* He took the pad back and wrote, *I guess I remind her of the tortoise when I'm up and moving.* He showed her what he'd written, then laughed.

"Why is Hidey's name spelled like that instead of H-e-i-d-i?" Joey asked as she tickled Sukari's ribs.

When we first got her she tried to hide from you know who. Sukari would look for her, signing "where hide cat?" He put his pencil down and signed each word for her, then wrote, *The name evolved into Hidey.*

When he showed Joey the signs, Sukari sat up and signed, WHERE HIDE CAT? and looked around. When she didn't see her, she signed, MORE TICKLE.

"No," the old man said. "That's enough tickle."

Sukari stood up and flailed her hands, then signed, MORE TICKLE, over and over.

"She's spoiled," he said. He started to write something, but Sukari grabbed his pad and threw it over the railing.

The old man signed something emphatically. "Tell her bad girl," he said to Joey. UNDERSTAND?

"Sukari's bad," Joey said, shaking a finger at her, but she couldn't keep from grinning.

Sukari marched back to Joey on her little bowed legs and bared her teeth.

The old man shouted, "Watch out," but Joey had no time to realize that the whisper she'd heard was a warning before Sukari bit her on the arm.

Joey's reaction was immediate. She caught Sukari's hand and bit her back.

Sukari screamed and ran to the old man, who smacked her bottom. "Are you okay?" he asked Joey.

She nodded. "She didn't break the skin. Besides, I get bitten all the time by our resident monster." Joey held out her arm for him to see. "Should I have bitten her back?"

His head bobbed. "That's exactly what you should have done."

Sukari crawled into his lap for sympathy and buried her face in her hands. When neither of them paid any attention, she peeked at her hand where Joey had bitten her, carefully parting the hairs to look for a wound. She held it up for the old man to examine, but he only scolded her again.

She signed, SORRY.

"Don't tell me, tell her you're sorry." He pointed to Joey.

Instead, she climbed him like a tree trunk, dropped over his shoulder and onto the slide, climbed to the top, and slid back down.

Joey went down the steps to retrieve the pad. She had so many questions.

Sukari pushed her hands between the old man's arm and his side, spread them, and watched Joey through the crack she'd created.

Joey wiped leaves from the pad and put it beside his foot. When she got back to the deck, she smiled, remembering not to show her teeth, and crooked a finger for Sukari to come.

GO. TELL SORRY, the man signed.

Sukari climbed down and moved cautiously toward Joey.

"Would she bite me again?"

He shook his head. "If you want her as a friend . . . ," he said to Sukari, then signed, WANT FRIEND, TELL SORRY.

Sukari turned, circled her chest with her small fist, and held her arm out, wrist bent, with the back of her hand to Joey.

The old man mimicked her bent wrist. He picked up the pad. *That's submissive behavior,* he scrawled in large letters and held it for Joey to see.

"No biting." She shook a finger at Sukari.

Sukari hung her head and signed something.

Joey waited to watch the old man's lips interpret. When he stopped laughing, he wrote, *She must really be sorry. She called herself "a dirty diaper devil."*

Joey laughed, then took Sukari's hand and pulled her into her lap. FRIEND, she signed. "Is that right?" she asked.

He gave her a thumbs-up.

"Did you buy her?" Joey asked.

He shook his head no, then began to write an explanation, some of which he crossed out. When he handed Joey the pad, a line was drawn through **bushmeat hunter.** Instead, he'd written, *A poacher killed her mother when she was just a few months old.*

Sukari was sitting in Joey's lap, facing the old man and letting Joey rub her belly.

"Oh no. Why?" Joey asked.

They ate her mother, the old man wrote, *and brought Sukari back to sell.*

"Ate her mother? Who eats chimpanzees?"

Chimpanzees are called bushmeat in Cameroon.

"Would they have eaten her, too?"

Not much meat on a baby, but they eat them if they're hungry enough. She'd already been sold to an amusement park. Joey watched his writing grow darker. *Others are sold to animal traders who in turn sell them to rich fools who collect wild animals as pets, or to research labs, where most of them end up anyway.*

Joey felt sick. "What would a research lab want with a baby chimpanzee?"

Chimps are genetically our closest relatives. Researchers use them to test all kinds of things including medicines before they're approved for use on humans.

"Don't you have to be sick before medicines work?"

They make them sick first.

"Even babies?"

That's not the half of it. They've been used in the space program, sent into orbit. . . . His face was getting red.

Joey changed the subject. "How did you get her?" She stroked Sukari's fingers with their perfect little nails.

The two sanctuaries for confiscated babies were full, so my wife and I took her. We were in Africa doing medical work and fell into doing some rehab with baby animals. When the rangers took her away from the amusement park owner, she was nearly dead, so they brought her to us. She's still small for her age, he added.

It took him a while to write his answer. "What's your name?" Joey asked before he finished.

SORRY, he signed, then wrote, *Dr. Mansell, Charles Mansell. Call me Charlie.*

Joey stuck her hand out and they shook. "My name's Joey. Joey Willis. I just live up the creek from here." She pointed. "We live where the old rest home used to be before it burned down."

"I remember it."

"Where's your wife?

"She died a year ago and I moved back here," he said, then looked away, out through the trees.

"I'm sorry," Joey said, and without really being aware of it, she signed SORRY at the same time.

Charlie saw it and wrote, *Fast learner.*

"I taught myself the alphabet," she said.

You weren't born deaf. How did you lose your hearing?

Joey wondered how he knew that. Without thinking, she touched one of the scars behind her ears. "I was sick," she said, without looking at him.

"How old were you?"

"Almost seven. How'd you know I wasn't born this way?"

If you'd been born deaf or lost it when you were very young, you wouldn't speak as clearly as you do. My mother was born deaf, and my father lost his hearing the same way you did but he was only two. Until they learned sign language, they had no language. Was it meningitis?

Joey nodded, then hugged Sukari. "May I come back to visit?"

"Any time," he said. *Any time,* he wrote, then added, *I was going to ask you. She needs someone young for company. Bring your brother.*

Joey hesitated. "I don't know whether my mother will let me do that. She's pretty nervous around animals. I don't think she likes them much."

That's too bad. Maybe we should come to your house so she can meet Sukari on home ground.

"Don't do that," Joey said too quickly. "I mean . . . I'd like for you to come over, and my stepfather would love to meet you, but I need to figure out how to tell Mom we met and all that first."

Charlie's eyes narrowed a bit but he nodded. "I understand."

It was a little after five and nearly dark when Joey straggled in, wet and cold. She'd wanted to give herself time to think about how she might tell her mother of meeting Charlie and Sukari, so she'd taken the long way home, coming through the deep woods of Jug Handle State Park, a thin strip of which formed the northern boundary of their property. She'd followed the familiar track uphill until it flattened out and became pygmy forest with its short, gnarled old cypress trees, rhododendrons, and dense thickets of huckleberries. Moisture clung to everything, and brushing through it had soaked her clothes.

Her mother met her at the door with the phone in her hand. "Where have you been? I was about to call the police."

Oh brother, Joey thought and rolled her eyes. If she told her she'd followed a strange man to his house and played with a chimpanzee, her mother would never let her out of her sight again. "I got turned around," she said.

Ruth shook the phone's antenna in her face. "I should never have let you go by yourself."

"I'm thirteen, Mom. Besides, I can't hear, I'm not blind. I just wasn't paying attention." She handed over the basket brimming with mushrooms, then went to stand with her back to the woodstove, palms held to the heat.

Ray sat in his chair reading the *Advocate-News* by the dim light of a hurricane lamp. He nodded at her and she nodded back. "There's a beefsteak in the basket."

His droopy mustache, which he kept long to cover bad teeth, bobbed.

Joey looked at her mother to repeat what he'd said, but she was sorting the mushrooms, bagging the dye ones into Ziplocs to freeze.

Joey smiled at Ray, then turned to face the woodstove.

She really liked Ray. He was nice to her mother and nice to her, but they'd long ago stopped trying to communicate. At first, he'd tried to write her notes, but he couldn't spell and Joey didn't read well enough then to solve the puzzle of his scrawled words. Though she'd since learned to decipher his notes, he rarely bothered anymore. It was easier to let Ruth interpret. Still, she felt an odd kinship with Ray. He'd lost the tips of the first two fingers on his left hand when a log slipped, trapping them against the post meant to hold logs on the truck. Joey often wondered if he could still feel them, phantoms like her mother's voice to her deaf ears. Though she'd wondered, she'd never asked. It had been enough just to feel that their losses gave them something in common. She looked at the two stubs supporting the newspaper and realized that after living in the same house for six years, she and Ray circled through the rooms like polite strangers. She'd spent the day actually talking with someone besides her mother, and it suddenly made her sad to think that she probably knew more about Charlie than she did about her stepfather.

"Ray," she said.

He glanced up. He frequently looked as if he was in pain, his brow a series of ridges so deep that they looked plowed into his forehead.

"Can you still feel the tips of your missing fingers?"

His mustache moved.

Joey looked at Ruth.

"He said, he does. All the time. Why'd you ask?"

Joey shrugged. "I just wondered."

The power suddenly came back on with a blaze of light as if

the room had exploded. Their cheers woke Luke from his nap on the couch. Ray blew out the hurricane lamp, turned the TV on to await the news, then went back to his paper.

Joey stayed by the woodstove with the hem of her shirt held out to catch the heat against her skin. She wasn't ready to lay aside the thrilling twist the day had taken. A few feet one way or the other and your whole life changed. She'd made a friend, two friends, and, in spite of her mother, she was going to learn to sign. She felt as if her world had just doubled in size.

She turned toward the kitchen, where her mother was slicing the beefsteak mushroom into strips like London broil. "Mom," she said.

"What?" Ruth asked, after waiting for Joey to continue.

"Nothing."

"What were you going to say?"

"Tell me again why you don't want me to learn sign language."

Ray lowered his paper.

Ruth leaned away from the stove and faced Joey, her brow creased. "I don't want to go into this again," she said. "What makes you ask?"

Ever since Smiley had taught her a few words, she'd wanted to learn sign language, but her mother had remained against it. Joey shrugged, turned to face the window, and smiled at her reflection in the glass. It was dark out, but in the glow of light from the house she could see that it was raining. She remembered the sound of rain on the aluminum roofs of trailers and wished she could recall its softer sound. "The water will be hot soon," she said. "I'm going to take a shower."

Chapter Three

Joey's legs twitched beneath the bedcovers like a dog's in a dream-chase. In her dream, she darted from behind a tree to the cover of another within a few feet of the cage where a baby Sukari lay curled into a fist-size ball, her white bottom tinted orange by the glow of the fire over which her mother cooked on a spit. A man, his face in shadow, sat in his undershirt, drinking a beer and watching the big chimpanzee turn slowly above the hot coals. Joey was close enough to reach the clasp on the cage door. But if the man saw her, he would chase, catch, and maybe kill her this time. Joey trembled in her hiding place, sick with fear. The man leaned into the light from the fire to poke the coals with the broken leg of a stool. His face, strange at first, began to redden from the heat until it seemed to bubble and melt, but when he leaned back, satisfied with the level of the flame, his features cooled and he looked like someone she knew. Joey gasped and jerked awake. Her vibrating alarm clock shuddered against her hip. She patted her pajama pocket and pushed the button down through the material, then removed the clock and put it on the nightstand. Her thumb was wet and wrinkled. She left her arm out in the chilly air to keep herself from falling back to sleep, afraid the dream would come again.

After a few minutes, when her arm felt frozen and the dream had faded, she rolled over and turned on the light beside her bed. It was still dark outside and she could see her reflection in the sliding glass doors. I-SEE-YOU, she signed to herself and grinned.

It was Friday. There'd been no school for four days because of the power outage, and though she really hated school, today she couldn't wait to get there and tell Roxy, her best friend, about Sukari and Charlie.

Last night, she'd had a hard time deciding what to wear. She'd draped her jeans and a brown sweater over the back of the chair near the woodstove before she went to bed, but now decided she wanted something else. She shivered as she stood in her closet trying to decide until finally the cold drove her to settle on a red V-neck, which was a good color on her but made her long neck look longer. She picked her red Converse All Stars to match her sweater, and yellow socks with red flowers. All dressed, she stopped to admire herself in the mirror and signed I-SEE-YOU again.

Mendocino coast winters were filled with short days, either rainy or clear and frosty. At this time of year the school day started before the sun came up, if it showed itself at all, and was not over until nearly dusk. Joey still disliked having to get up so early. Until two years ago, she'd been home-schooled, keeping her mother's hours and learning her lessons during the slow times at a table in a windowless corner of the Old Dock Café.

Going to work with her mother was a habit that started in Reno. Ruth never left her at home or alone with anyone until she started first grade. After she went deaf, they were never apart and Ruth took over her education.

It was when Luke became too much for his babysitter to handle that home-schooling came to an end. His sitter, Mrs. Gomez, lived in the trailer park that surrounded the café and hers was the one directly across from the restaurant. Once Luke discovered how to break out of her little fenced-in yard and visit Ruth at will, it became impossible to get anything done. Her mother finally gave up and Joey entered a public school for the second time in her life as a seventh-grader.

For most of that year, Joey had been miserable. Worse than being the only deaf student, she was tall for her age and twig-thin, with so much hair that she thought she looked like one of those long-handled brushes her mother used to clear cobwebs from the ceiling. The only thing she liked about her looks were her eyes. They were as black as the trout pond in the woods behind their house, and her lashes were long.

Her feelings of isolation were more intense in the crowded school than they ever were at home with only her mother to talk to, or even in the quiet little café with its Spanish-speaking cook and an owner who only nodded and smiled at her.

She'd been reading her mother's lips forever, even before she was deaf. When she was little, Ruth read to her every night, but they weren't allowed to talk out loud when *he* was home, so her mother taught her to read locked in the bathroom, whispering every word.

Joey had done well with her lessons when her mother taught her, but once in school, she had a terrible time. It was too easy for teachers and the other students to forget she was deaf, not to face her when they spoke to her, but even when they did, she found their lips difficult, often impossible, to read. When she tried to explain her poor grades to her mother, Ruth said she wasn't trying hard enough and called the school to make sure Joey was using their FM system.

Picking up the loaner FM system was Joey's first stop every morning. To hear her teachers, she had to carry a microphone from class to class for them to wear on a cord around their necks and two boxy little amplifiers that she wore strapped to her chest like little square breasts. Worse, the headphones were big and bulbous and her auburn hair flared up on either side of the wide headband. Someone said she looked like a praying mantis and the nickname "bug-head" caught on and stuck.

The hardest part about being home-schooled had been not having friends, but when she got to school, she discovered that she was shy to the point of having sweaty palms. And she was too hard to talk to and written notes were too slow. For the first year and a half, she moved through the days alone, ticking off the classes in long, lead-filled minutes.

It wasn't until last month, after the Christmas break, when Roxanne arrived at school, that Joey made her first real friend. Roxanne was what her mother would have called a "live wire," and by the end of her first week everyone called her Roxy. Roxy's mother was deaf, so her first language was sign. She immediately made Joey her best friend.

Telling Roxy about Sukari wasn't the only thing on Joey's

mind while she waited for the bus. She was thinking about Kenny, the new boy in her biology class. His lips, like Roxy's, were easy to read and he always smiled when he saw her. Most boys either ignored her or teased her but Kenny did neither.

On the bus ride to school, Joey practiced the alphabet by signing the letters of license plates with her hand in her coat pocket so no one would see her. Her mother worked Saturdays and she wondered if tomorrow would be too soon to go back to visit Sukari. It probably was, she decided. She didn't want to make a pest of herself.

As the bus pulled in, she saw Kenny standing on the front steps with two other boys. When he smiled, her face flushed crimson. She raised her hand though not high enough to be called a real wave. When the boys he was with grinned and elbowed him, she ducked her head and went in the other entrance.

Over the Christmas holidays, the school had removed all the lockers and painted the walls beige on top and a gloomy gray on the bottom. Entering through the double doors continued to startle her, as if the job had been freshly done during the night. But she liked the change; it added room to the corridors. Before, stepping into the narrow halls was like being caught in an undertow. Now there were walls to hug but the color made what often felt like prison look like prison.

She went to the office to sign out the FM system, then to the library to return a book. While there, she wandered over to see if *her* sign language book was still there. It was, along with a new one called *Signs of the Times*. She took it down and looked to see if anyone had ever checked it out. No one had. Joey saw other students begin to leave the library. The first bell must

have rung. She quickly looked up the sign for "name" in the index. With her back to anyone who might be watching, she tried
out, MY NAME J-O-E-Y, then put the book back on the shelf.

The door to her first classroom was still locked so she
walked to the glass doors at the end of the corridor. Roxy and
her boyfriend were talking to Dillon and Kristin at a picnic
table outside the cafeteria. Joey stepped back so they wouldn't
see her watching.

Brad, Roxy's boyfriend, was sitting in the center at one end
of the table, swinging his legs. Roxy tried to sit beside him,
but he leaned toward her, blocking her way. She whirled and
stomped a foot, then grabbed his arm and tried to pull him off
the table. They wrangled until Dillon nudged Brad and jerked
his head toward the breezeway between the two buildings.
Joey thought for a second he'd seen her at the window, until,
out of the corner of her eye, she saw Harley coming along the
sidewalk in his motorized wheelchair. Harley wasn't his real
name; it was the nickname some kids had given him. He was in
the eighth grade and had cerebral palsy.

Brad hopped off the table and loped toward him. He caught
the chair by the armrests and stopped it before Harley could
steer around him. Joey saw Harley yell at Brad, who let him go.
Harley started forward again with a little jerk but Brad hopped
in front of him. Harley stopped. Brad jumped aside. Harley
started up again. Roxy and Kristin were laughing. Joey bit her
lip, turned, and walked back to her classroom. Kenny was in her
biology class, but first there was English. She had an hour before
she'd see him again.

When the teacher came and unlocked the door, Joey took

the amplifiers from her backpack and followed Ms. Rowe into the room.

"How are you, Joey?"

"Good, thanks." Joey handed her the microphone with its neck cord, then took a seat in the rear corner. It was the most popular table, away from the center of things, and Joey knew to get there early or miss out on one of the four seats. She took the one facing Ms. Rowe. The room began to fill.

Kristin, Cindee, and Jason sat with her. Jason said, "What's happening?"

"Nothing much," Joey answered.

When they all laughed and Kristin slapped Jason's shoulder, Joey knew that he hadn't said "what's happening" out loud. He'd only mouthed the words. This was a favorite trick to play on her. She smiled and put her headphones on.

Cindee opened a bag of Starburst candies and slid one across the table to each of them.

"Thanks," Joey said.

Kristin examined the nails on her left hand while she shook a bottle of nail polish with the other.

Ms. Rowe took roll, then clapped for their attention. *Chapter 3,* she wrote on the board, then held up the paperback of Steinbeck's *The Pearl* and *The Red Pony.* They'd finished *The Pearl* a week ago. "Who wants to start?" she said.

Everyone laughed and turned to look at Joey. Kristin tapped one bulb of her headset with a newly polished fingernail. "You're too loud," she said.

Joey blushed and adjusted the volume.

Ms. Rowe blew in the microphone. "Can you still hear me?"

Joey nodded, though she couldn't. The volume was too low, but she didn't want to go through trying to find the level that she could hear but the rest of the room couldn't. Besides, they were going to take turns reading, so she didn't need to hear.

Terry got picked first. Joey slouched in her chair and read to herself. When Cindee tapped her shoulder, Joey had just started chapter 4. "It's your turn," she said.

Joey's heart started to pound. Her teachers told her she read better than anyone in class, but she hated reading aloud because she knew her voice sounded funny. She found herself getting tangled up, as if she were reading with one eye and watching the class to see if she was pronouncing the words correctly with the other. She looked at Ms. Rowe, who was tapping on the microphone.

"Isn't this working?"

Joey turned the volume up.

Kids giggled and plugged their ears. She turned it down again.

Jason reached, pulled the scrunchie off Kristin's ponytail, and put it on his wrist like a bracelet. Kristin tried to grab it back. Joey's attention was scattered, distracted by Kristin and Jason and trying to understand where they were in the book.

Ms. Rowe wrote on the board, **4th paragraph, page 166.**

Joey flipped back to 166 and counted down. "The fifteenth of January came, and the colt was not born," she read, then glanced at Jason. He had Kristin's and his hand joined at the wrist with the scrunchie. "And the twentieth came; a lump of fear began . . ." Over the top of the book, Joey saw Jason's nostrils flare and his head bob from side to side. Kristin kicked him. Cindee, who had borrowed Kristin's polish, giggled behind her hand with its wet purple nails. Jason was imitating the nasal sound of Joey's voice. She swallowed and found her place. ". . . a lump of fear began to form in Jody's stomach. 'Is it all right?' he demanded of Billy," she continued, pronouncing each word as carefully as she could, plodding along as if she were slow-witted.

She stopped and looked up when Jason made a throat-cutting motion.

"That was fine," Ms. Rowe said, then pointed to Jason. "You next," she said, smiling coldly.

Joey sank back into the chair and stared at the page. It blurred and swam before her eyes. *Don't let them see you sweat,* her mother's voice said in time to the dull thud of a headache coming.

Next period was biology. Kenny glanced at her when he came in. She felt herself start to blush and quickly looked away. She'd put her backpack on the empty seat at her table. When Kenny headed in her direction, she leaned to move it, but Dillon caught his arm and dragged him off to sit with him.

Their teacher, Mr. Cary, was working his way, though not in any regular order, through the phyla in the animal, plant, and fungi kingdoms. They had started with marine invertebrates and algae while the weather was still nice enough to visit tide pools, then they'd switched to amphibians and fungi when the rains started in November. Joey drew well and had made cards with hand-colored sketches of each organism on one side and a description and some characteristics on the other to use as flash cards. Her best grades ever were in this class.

"Do you have your aids?" Mr. Cary asked. She hadn't given him the microphone because she tried never to wear the FM system in front of Kenny. He knew she was deaf but she wanted at least to look normal.

Joey shrugged. "I forgot them," she lied.

Jason glanced at her and grinned.

"Today-is-a-lecture-class," Mr. Cary said slowly. "Do-you-want-someone-to-take-notes-for-you?"

Joey wanted to slide under the table. She shook her head. "I can do it."

Mr. Cary was no longer looking at her. "Thanks, Ken," he said.

Joey glanced at Kenny, who smiled.

"Ken-said-he-would-take-notes-for-you."

Joey blushed.

At lunch, when she got to the cafeteria, Roxy was already there with Brad, Kristin, and Dillon. Joey was almost at the end of the line and had raised her hand to wave, when Roxy turned away sharply. Well, that was okay. Joey understood. She wanted to be with her boyfriend, and Joey didn't really like Kristin and Dillon that much, anyway. She'd wait to tell Roxy about Sukari this afternoon in history, their one class together. She took her sandwich and left the cafeteria. She had a place behind the library where she used to go and eat before Roxy was her friend.

"Where were you?" Roxy asked her when she flopped into the desk beside her in history.

"When?"

"At lunch. I saved you a seat."

"I . . . I didn't see you," Joey said.

Roxy shrugged.

Their teacher rapped for attention. History was Joey's worst subject. It was nearly all lecture and she couldn't keep up. Roxy had volunteered to take notes for her, but her notes were so bad that they were nearly useless.

Roxy slipped her a note: *There's a dance next Saturday. Are you going?*

Roxy knew she wasn't going. Sometimes she did stuff like that, ask a question she knew the answer to. Joey wasn't sure why.

I've been invited to a friend's house, she wrote back, stretching the truth a little since they'd set no specific date. *He has a . . .* Joey stopped and crossed the last part out. Something warned her not to go any further. As much as she wanted to share meeting Sukari with Roxy, she couldn't get the way she'd laughed when Brad was teasing Harley out of her mind. She suddenly decided it wasn't a secret that would be safe with Roxy.

Roxy lived with her mother in a small apartment in a building that overlooked Noyo Harbor. Since the day they'd met Joey had been planning to take Roxy to the café to meet Ruth. *How about coming down to meet my mother tomorrow?*

Roxy reached across the aisle and scribbled, *Can we eat free?*

Joey smiled and nodded. Roxy was her mother's link to the world, as Ruth was Joey's. How could they not like each other?

At home that night, she was less sure. "I thought I'd bring Roxy down to meet you tomorrow." Joey was setting the table.

"I'd like to meet one of your little friends," Ruth said. "Which one is she?"

Joey hated it when her mother acted as if she were still a child and that her life was normal. "She's not little, she's my only friend, and I told you about her; her mother's deaf," Joey said sharply.

"Watch your tone of voice, young lady."

"That'll be a tall order," Joey said, pulling on an earlobe.

"What's with you?" her mother snapped.

"Nothing. It's just you act as if I'm armpit deep in friends and beating boyfriends off with a stick."

"You're too young for a boyfriend."

"Are you even listening to me?"

"I said yes. I'd like to meet her. What more do you want?"

"Nothing. Nothing at all."

The next day, Joey rode to work with her mother and spent the morning trying to study in her old corner, but she was too excited to get anything done. When her stomach began to growl, Joey decided it was time to go get Roxy.

She walked North Harbor Drive to the base of the staircase behind the Harbor Lite Motel. The climb was steep, at least 150 feet, and by the time she reached the top, she'd stripped down to her T-shirt. She walked the block and a half to Roxy's apartment building and knocked on the door. Though it was nearly twelve, Roxy answered still in her pajamas.

"Did you forget?" Joey asked.

Roxy stepped out onto the catwalk and pulled the door closed behind her. "I can't go. My mother's on a tear."

"Come on. Let me ask her. You can have whatever you want for lunch and ice cream and my mother will bring you home when she gets off at three."

Roxy turned her head sharply, listening. "Well, that suits me, too, old lady," she yelled through the crack in the door.

Joey flinched. "My mother'd kill me if I yelled at her like that."

"My mother'd kill me, too, if she could hear me." Roxy grinned. "She just said she doesn't care where I go. So wait here. I'll change clothes."

Joey sat on the top step. A whale-watching boat lay off the harbor entrance, waiting to surf the next breaker through the narrow opening to the channel. The passengers weren't looking too healthy; many were still hanging over the railing. A storm was due by nightfall and the seas were getting higher by the hour.

"Have you ever seen a whale?" Joey asked Roxy as they walked toward the staircase.

"Just ole Arnold, that blimp in our history class?"

"He's real nice, though," Joey said.

Joey had never told Roxy that the reason she didn't sign was because her mother didn't want her to. She hadn't wanted to go into the reasons, all of which would have been offensive to someone who learned to sign before she learned to speak.

After Joey introduced them, the first thing out of Roxy's mouth, when she shook hands with Ruth, was, "I'm going to teach Joey to sign."

From the look on her mother's face, you'd have thought she'd said she was going to teach Joey to rob banks. "I don't want her signing," Ruth said.

"She thinks I'm better off reading lips," Joey said, trying to change the footing they were on, though she knew it was too late.

One of the reasons Roxy had been instantly popular at school was that she would say or do anything. The first words she taught Joey to sign were four-letter. Nothing was sacred. Roxy pulled herself up to her full height, looked Ruth right in the eye, and said, "Well, that's really stupid."

Ruth's eyes narrowed. "My daughter. My decision. I wish I could say it had been a pleasure to meet you." She spun and walked away.

When Roxy slammed out of the restaurant, Joey started to follow, but Ruth caught up with her at the door and grabbed her arm. "Don't you dare follow that little . . . snot."

"Why were you so mean to her? She's my friend."

"Not anymore, she's not."

Joey jerked free of her mother and ran out the door. Roxy was marching back down North Harbor Drive toward the cliff and the staircase. Joey called to her, but she kept going.

When Joey spoke in normal tones, she couldn't hear herself. "Roxy, wait," she screamed.

Roxy kept going.

Joey took off running and caught her at the base of the staircase. "Please, don't be mad at me. You're my best friend."

Roxy turned and for a moment Joey thought she was going to hit her. Her hands were balled into fists and her jaw was set. "Your mother's an idiot," she snapped.

Joey couldn't bring herself to say *I know she is* and yet she was afraid to disagree with Roxy. She lowered her head and nodded.

When Roxy started up the stairs, Joey thought that was it. She'd lost her one and only friend. She squeezed her eyes shut against the sting of tears and turned away, but she'd gone only a few yards back toward the restaurant when Roxy tapped her shoulder. "I'm sorry," she said, when Joey spun around. "She is an idiot, but let's not let that stand in our way." Roxy hugged her. "I am going to teach you to sign, in spite of her. How 'bout it?"

The relief Joey felt was overwhelming. Her head bobbed. "Oh, yes, please."

Luke was picking up Spanish from Mrs. Gomez, and it occurred to Joey, as she and Roxy worked in the library on Monday with *Signs of the Times* open between them, that if she taught Luke to sign, starting now, he'd pick it up as quickly as Spanish and be able to sign with Sukari when they met. Before she and Roxy left for history class, Joey checked the *Signed English Dictionary for Preschool and Elementary Levels* out of the library and sneaked it home in her backpack.

That evening, after dinner, when Joey thought her mother was out helping Ray stack the firewood he'd split, she told Luke she had a game to teach him. They were sitting on the floor in his room, forming the signs for "want candy" with his hands, when her mother walked in.

"Want candy," Luke shouted, then signed, WANT CANDY, for Ruth and giggled.

Joey's stomach did a flip-flop as she watched the expression on her mother's face go from pleasure at seeing Joey reading to Luke, to a tight-jawed, icy stare. She marched out of the room and came back with a pen and notebook, something she did whenever she considered what she had to say too important for Joey to miss a word. She'd already written, *It's okay to teach him some words for fun but I don't want you two talking with your hands. It makes your handicap more obvious.*

Like an ember in a dead-looking fire, resentment flared. "More obvious than hearing aids?" Joey snapped.

Her mother wrote something and poked the pad for her to

read on. *It could stunt . . .* she dashed a line through "stunt" and wrote, *slow down his learning to talk. He's already mixing his English with Spanish.*

Ruth snatched back the pad and added, *And it will keep you from fitting in with people who can hear!*

"How am I gonna fit in with the hearing, with only you to talk to, Mom?"

"Practice your lip-reading," Ruth said, emphasizing each word. "And stay away from that awful little girl," she snapped. "She's trash."

Joey opened her mouth to argue, but her mother gave her the *look,* jaw set, scarred eyebrow arched. The *look* threatened the silent treatment, which would disconnect Joey completely. She knew the sound of her mother's voice was only a memory, but even so, she couldn't risk being cut off from the only human sound she could still hear. She'd be a crab in a jar then.

When they first came to Fort Bragg, her mother had tried to make their homelessness an adventure. They'd parked someplace different each night, as if they were camping. Joey never went to Glass Beach without remembering the night they'd slept there.

For decades, Glass Beach had been the city dump and over the years since it closed, the ocean had broken up the glass jars and bottles and worn the shards down to small, smooth, jewel-like fragments. Ruth had sat on the sand and watched Joey select little pieces of the colorful glass to keep for a souvenir. Nearby, a little boy was collecting hermit crabs from an exposed tide pool. He had four or five of them in a jar when he put the lid on and carried them over to show Joey. When she saw them circling and circling, their tiny pincers feeling for a way out, she tried to take them away from him. He started to cry and Ruth made Joey give back the jar.

"Make him let 'em go, Mommy," Joey cried. "Make him let them go."

"They're his, Joey," her mother said.

Joey tried to grab the jar again. The little boy ran with it to his mother.

"Mommy," Joey screamed, "make him let 'em go."

"I can't, Joey." Ruth picked her up and tried to carry her away, but she screamed and kicked, pleading for the crabs.

"Joey, stop it. What's the matter with you?"

Joey caught her mother's face between her hands. "Mommy, they can't hear in there."

Tears came to her mother's eyes. She turned and marched back across the sand to the little boy and his mother to explain that Joey was deaf and that she was afraid that the little crabs couldn't hear in that jar. The boy's mother's indignant expression softened and she promised that he'd let them go before they went home.

That night, after her mother had forbidden her to see Roxy again, Joey lay on her bed staring at the ceiling, tears running in a steady stream from her eyes into her ears. The only person Joey had ever trusted completely was her mother and she felt like Ruth was pulling away. She couldn't understand why adding Roxy, Charlie, and Sukari to her life might mean breaking the bond she and her mother had. Since she'd understood about the crabs, why couldn't she understand now?

Chapter Four

Wednesday was speech therapy and the one day her mother still picked her up, though at the hospital, where her therapist was, rather than at school. Since she hadn't taken the bus home, it was still early when Joey jumped from the car at the top of their driveway to collect the mail. As far as she could remember, she'd never received a letter or even a card, though there were a few in a shoebox from her grandmother who died when she was five. Joey handed the stack through her mother's window without looking at it. It was while she was getting plates down to set the table for dinner that her mother tapped her shoulder and handed her the envelope.

"For you," she said with a frown.

Joey turned it over and read her name and address. It gave her a strange sense of herself, as if she'd become an adult for the price of a postage stamp.

Ms. Joey Willis
19904 Morgan Creek Dr.
Ft. Bragg, CA 95437

She looked for a return address but there was only the name Mansell.

Having missed the chance to tell her mother about meeting Charlie and Sukari, she now found, with this letter in her hand, that she'd gone back to wanting to keep them a secret, but her mother waited expectantly. Joey stared again at her name and address, then put the envelope in the pocket of her sweater and began to set the table.

Her mother waved her hand in front of Joey's face. "Who's Mansell?"

"A person down on Turner."

Joey started to turn away but her mother caught her chin. "A man, a woman, a child?"

Joey couldn't hear her tone of voice but her mother's face showed signs of growing anger.

"A man," Joey said. "An old man. A doctor."

"How did you meet him?"

"I was mushrooming on his property by accident."

"Why would he write you a letter?"

Joey's knees felt weak. "Because I'm deaf, Mom," she snapped. "It's hard to talk to me." In that instant she knew why she wanted to keep their meeting from her mother. Charlie was going to be the one person with whom she wouldn't feel ashamed of her deafness. He, unlike her mother, understood how she felt. And Joey knew that Roxy would tire of teaching her to sign, but Charlie wouldn't.

"That doesn't answer my question. Why is he writing you?"

"I don't know. I haven't read it yet." She stared boldly back at her mother, but her stomach filled with butterflies. She wasn't going to lose him to her mother's suspicions and secret-keeping. She was thinking just that when Ruth snatched the plates away. "I think you should let me see it."

"No. It's mine. You can't read my mail." Joey whirled, headed for her room, but changed her mind, circled the sofa, and ran from the house.

She ran at first as if her mother were on her heels, then zigged and zagged up through the trees behind their house. About fifty yards up a slope, on the top terrace of their property, was the stump of a redwood tree that had grown there long before Columbus discovered America. The stump was over twelve feet across and had a burned-out hollow beneath it. When they'd first moved to this house, Joey, unsure of the kind of man Ray would be, found and kept the location of the tree a secret in case she ever needed to hide again. Now it was just her place to be alone.

On either side of the stump was a rectangular springboard hole where the loggers, who cut the tree in the early 1900s, before chainsaws were invented, plunged the end of a thick board into each side of its trunk. She'd seen pictures of men standing on these platforms, one on either end of a double-handled saw, cutting the tree off four feet or so above the ground. By putting a foot in one of the springboard holes, Joey could boost herself up onto the wide, flat top.

In the winter, she kept a small brown tarp hidden in the dry center of the hollow. Joey bent to retrieve it and felt the hair on her neck prickle. She whirled around, her heart racing, but as usual there was no one there. Sometimes silence gave her the creeps, especially in dim light with anger in the air.

She shook the daddy longlegs out of the tarp and pried the banana slugs off with a twig, then spread it across the soggy, spongy cushion of redwood leaves that blanketed the stump. She climbed up to sit with her back against one of the two trees that grew from the roots of the ancient redwood. She dug the letter from her pocket and peeled it open as carefully as she opened gifts at Christmas.

Dear Joey,

I wanted to write and apologize once again for the way I behaved when we met. With all the rain we've had, mushroom hunters have been traipsing in and out of here with little or no regard for the damage they do. I never collect them myself. They all look dangerously the same to me, but I love them and from now on shall depend on you to tell me which ones are good to eat. I admire you knowing the difference.

Also, I hope I didn't upset you by ranting on the issue of research labs using chimps like hairy test tubes. Once you get to know Sukari and see how closely her thoughts and feelings match ours, testing on them becomes as intolerable as slavery is to us now. Those without voices, politically or literally, risk terrible suffering.

Anyway, I'm really writing to invite you to visit anytime. Sukari pouted for hours after you left and only relented after a bribe of an apple, two Oreo cookies, and a box of raisins—her favorite.

I went to the bookstore yesterday and ordered a present for you. It will be here by the end of next week. In the meantime, why don't you come visit us on Saturday if you haven't other plans. You are still welcome to bring your mother and your brother. I'm sure she'll be fine, once she meets Sukari. If it's nice, we could go mushrooming, then have a picnic on the deck.

I thought I'd tell you a little about my parents and about living in Africa, but I'm quite tired now. Maybe you could think of questions you'd like answered.

If Saturday is not convenient, just stop in anytime.

Sincerely,
Charles Mansell and

 *Sukari*

Joey read and reread her letter. She ran her finger over Sukari's scribbled signature. This was the first invitation to anything that she had ever gotten, except to places with her mother and Ray. Whenever they went to someone's house for a dinner party, they took a dish. Potlucks were a tradition on the coast. She wondered what she could bring to their picnic and what she would tell her mother. *Bananas,* she thought, suddenly. *I can buy them in the cafeteria . . . and apples and Oreos and a box of raisins. I won't have to tell Mom anything.*

She carefully folded the tarp and placed her letter in the center of it before tucking it back into the hollow. When she turned around, Luke was trudging up the slope toward her.

"Are you a bear coming to eat me?" She trembled with mock fear.

Luke motioned for her to come, then turned to start back down the hill.

Joey cupped a hand over her right ear. "What'd ya say, bear?"

Luke turned and grinned, then humped his shoulders, held his arms away from his sides, and hulked toward her.

Joey covered her mouth with the back of her hand as if to stifle a scream. "Help. Lord help me," she cried when Luke's eyes narrowed and his pudgy little jaw set.

"Grrrrrr."

"Please don't eat me, Mr. Bear," Joey pleaded. "I'll give you honey if you won't eat me."

Luke stopped and straightened. "No honey," he shouted.

"Oh yes, honey," Joey said. "That's what you need to make you a nice bear."

Luke turned to run, his short legs pumping.

Joey charged down the hill and scooped him up before they reached the bottom of the slope. She kissed the back of his neck, making slurping sounds, while Luke bucked like a pony to get away. "Honey for a bad bear."

Luke screeched to be let go.

Joey put him down and gave chase when he started to run again, but slowly so that he could beat her to the back door, which he locked once he was inside. Joey twisted the knob, calling, "Let me in, Mr. Bear, let me in," until her mother appeared at the window in the door, pulled Luke away, and un-locked it.

Her mother's face was still pinched with anger. She pointed to Joey's place at the table, then turned away without saying a word—for Joey, the ultimate punishment.

The plates, silverware, and place mats were still stacked in the center of the table. Joey ignored her mother's direction and began to set each place, but her mother caught her by the shoulder, took the plates from her, and again pointed to her chair.

"Why are you mad at me?" Joey asked.

Her mother's face reddened. "It's dangerous to keep se-crets," she snapped. "Why would an old man write to you? He might be a pervert, or something."

"He's not a pervert. He's just a nice old man."

"How do you know?"

Joey shrugged. It was her take on him, that was all. She'd known kind people and cruel people and there was a differ-ence she could almost smell. "And even if he is a pervert, I'm taller than he is and he's weak and sickly," she said, taking a seat at the end of the table where she could see the TV. Since she couldn't follow the conversation at dinner, at least she could practice her lip-reading watching the newscasters.

On Saturday morning, Joey woke at first light and checked her thumbs for dampness. They were dry. She smiled and rolled over to see what kind of day it would be. If it was going to be sunny, it was too early to tell. She wanted sun. She wanted to mushroom hunt and picnic. She'd spent the last of her allowance on apples, bananas, Oreos, and raisins for Sukari, and stashed them in her backpack, ready to go, along with her list of questions.

When she came into the kitchen, her mother was just lighting the stove. She turned and smiled. "You're up early."

"So are you. Are you working today?"

Ruth shook her head, adjusted the flame under the frying pan, then turned back to Joey. "It's supposed to be sunny for a while. Thought I'd take Luke to the beach, let him out to run." She grinned. "How 'bout it?"

Joey loved going to the beach with her brother, and her mother knew it. "I—I can't," she stammered.

"Why not?"

"I have to . . . too much homework."

Though she did lots of homework just to keep up, Joey had never claimed to have too much to go to the beach. A V of suspicion formed between her mother's brows.

"What kind of homework?"

For a moment Joey couldn't think of anything. "General stuff," she said, then remembered that she had chosen a mushroom project for her midterm science paper, similar to what her mother had done in her college mushroom class. "I'm going to start my science project," she added, leaving out that it wasn't due for a month and a half.

"What kind of project?"

"I want to make spore prints like you did," she said, "and use them to identify mushroom families."

Her mother looked pleased. She finished breaking eggs into

the pan, added Tabasco and a little milk, then began to scramble them. "Do you have the paper ---------- them on and ---------- preserve them ----------?"

Joey missed part of the question but got the gist because she already knew she'd need small squares of paper with half-black, half-white circles, and squares of clear plastic to cover the powdery prints once the spores dropped. "I was hoping you had all that stuff somewhere, or I could make the circles with a Magic Marker."

"I may have. I'll check in a minute," her mother said, dividing the eggs between three large plates and a small one. She shouted for Ray, then handed a plate to Joey, but didn't let go. "I forgot to ask, did you want eggs?"

"Sure," Joey said, a little too eagerly. But before her mother had time to realize that her enthusiasm for eggs was just relief that her fibbing seemed to have worked, she grabbed a clean fork from the drain-board and headed for the table.

Lugging mushroom-hunting paraphernalia and her backpack full of fruit, cookies, and raisins, Joey climbed the steps to Charlie's deck and knocked on the sliding glass door. Sukari's face appeared at the lower edge of the drapes. When she saw Joey, she grinned and signed, I-SEE-YOU. She began to twirl around, rolling herself up tightly in the curtains like a sausage.

"I hope now's okay," Joey said, when Charlie opened the door to let her in.

His hands flashed in welcome. FINE, FINE. "Now is fine. Come in."

Charlie had picked Sukari up, drapery and all, before open-ing the door. "Ready?" he asked, before unfurling her.

Joey put her stuff on the floor and nodded.

Sukari came rolling out and scrambled into Joey's arms. HUG, HURRY, HUG, she signed.

Charlie indicated with a raised finger that he'd be right back, then folded his three middle fingers into his palm and held his thumb to his ear and his pinky to his mouth. "I'm on the phone," he said and went into his library, where he picked the receiver off the desk. The house had a pleasant musty smell, as if the old books in the floor-to-ceiling case that lined the wall were baking in the overheated house. More books rose in stacks on the floor. Papers were scattered everywhere, as if all the doors and windows had been left open during the last storm.

Sukari leaned back so Joey could see her hands and signed something, practically brushing Joey's nose.

SORRY, Joey signed. "I don't know WHAT you're saying."

Sukari signed again, then descended to the floor and swag-gered into the office looking a lot like Luke as Mr. Bear. When she pulled on Charlie's pants leg and signed, BOOK, he clamped the receiver between his left cheek and his shoulder, freeing his hands to sift through a pile of papers on his desk, where he found a book and handed it to her. Sukari scampered back, took Joey's hand, and led her to the sofa.

She climbed into Joey's lap and opened her animal alphabet book. "A" was an alligator. Sukari signed, TEETH BAD, and covered her eyes with her hands. She did, COW, then, DRINK

GOOD, before scooting off the sofa and running to the refrigerator. She tugged at the handle, reached up, and pulled on the padlock. She turned and signed something Joey couldn't interpret, then, WANT DRINK. Sukari suddenly looked past Joey, who turned around to see Charlie standing in the office doorway, the phone still clamped between his ear and his shoulder. SUKARI BAD, FRIEND GO, he signed.

Sukari slinked back to the couch and climbed up to sit beside Joey again. She turned a page and signed, DOG, then, BITE SUKARI, and covered the picture with both hands and glanced at Charlie. He had turned back to his desk. She flipped the pages to "T" and poked the picture of a turtle. "What is that?" Joey asked, just as she did when reading to Luke.

Sukari made a fist with her thumb on top then draped the cupped palm of her right hand over the fist, leaving her thumb to protrude like the head of a turtle. When Joey made the same sign, Sukari signed, GOOD GIRL, then jumped off the sofa and ran down the hall. A moment later she was back. COME HURRY, she signed and grabbed Joey's hand to pull her along.

Sukari's room made Luke's look orderly. Fat hemp ropes, probably scavenged from the harbor, crisscrossed it at various heights and angles and gave the place a slightly fishy smell. Toys littered the floor: balls of different sizes and colors, a dozen stuffed animals, a tricycle, a red wagon, a set of drums, a horn, a xylophone with color-coded keys, and a playpen turned upside down. A plastic chair swung on a chain from the ceiling. Her bed was a mattress with a pillow and blanket on a platform built near the ceiling.

Sukari scrambled through the debris and climbed onto a chair beside the large aquarium beneath her window. She pointed at the abalone shell on the gravel bottom of the tank and signed, TURTLE.

"That's not a turtle, silly," Joey said. "That's a seashell."

Sukari drew her lips back and shook her arms. TURTLE HIDE, she signed.

Joey grinned. "If that's a turtle, where are its head and legs?"

Sukari jumped up and down.

"Okay, okay." Joey lifted the abalone shell. Beneath it was Sukari's tortoise in a hibernating torpor. I-SEE TURTLE, Joey signed.

From across the room came a flash of light. Joey looked up. Charlie had taken their picture with a Polaroid. He pulled the print from the front of the camera, glanced at his watch, then weaved through the chaos with his notepad on which he'd already written, *Shall we go for a walk now? It's supposed to rain later.*

"Sure." Joey grinned at him. "I signed a sentence."

"I saw that."

Charlie held off Sukari's attempts to grab the picture. "Behave," he snapped, before pulling the developed print from its backing.

He had caught Sukari standing on the chair, her hands forming the sign for "turtle," her lips pursed as if blowing out candles, and Joey beside her holding the abalone shell in the air and smiling. Joey stared at the picture. How could she have imagined this moment? Would Roxy or anyone else believe her if she told them that she had a sign-language-using chimpanzee for a friend? "It's wonderful," she said, and moved to hand it back to Charlie.

He pushed it back. "It's for you."

Joey wanted to keep it more than anything, but where? It was too valuable to hide in her damp hollow tree, and her mother would find it anyplace else. "Could you keep it for me for a while?"

Charlie's brow creased, then his eyebrows bobbed. "Did you tell your mother about meeting us?"

Joey missed everything but "tell" and "mother," all she really needed to see.

She nodded her head. "She knows I met you; she asked about the letter, but I didn't tell her about Sukari." She stopped there and hoped that he'd let it go. Her mother *was* silly about animals, but it had dawned on Joey that if she found out Sukari signed, it would give her just the ammunition she needed. Ruth had convinced herself that sign language was shorthand for real language. If she knew a chimpanzee used it, that would seal it for Joey.

As if he'd read her mind, *Still, secrets aren't good,* he wrote. *They just make people think there is something to hide even if there isn't.*

Joey picked Sukari up. "I know. I'll tell her," she said, hugging the little chimp. "Do you want to see where I live?" Joey asked Sukari.

When Charlie signed, GO WALK. SEE FRIEND HER HOUSE, Sukari squirmed out of Joey's arms, ran to the front door, signed, HURRY, HURRY, then climbed the coat rack and tried to put her coat on without taking it off the hanger.

Joey led the way along a fairly level Jug Handle State Park trail so that Charlie didn't have to climb any slopes. Sukari rode draped over Joey's head, a foot on each shoulder, her arms locked under Joey's chin. Before they left, Charlie had asked her if she enjoyed birds, and when she said she did but didn't know the different kinds, he'd loaned her a pair of binoculars and brought along a field guide to western birds.

Joey's sharpened senses let her spot the telltale movements of birds before Sukari or Charlie saw them. She'd point them out and he'd find them for her in the field guide: two Stellar's jays, a Varied thrush, a half-dozen Chestnut-backed chickadees, Oregon juncos, and an Acorn woodpecker. When they flushed a covey of quail, which flew into trees like a barrel load of bowling balls, Sukari screamed and jumped from Joey's shoulders onto Charlie's back.

BIRD BIRD. "You big sissy." Charlie clicked her under the chin.

Joey took Sukari back from Charlie so that he was free to write. Something about having him for a friend made her feel like a baby bird teetering on the edge of its nest, craving flight. She took Sukari's hands in hers, spread their arms, and swooped down a small hill, around a tree, and back up to join Charlie.

They walked a bit farther until Charlie stopped and put a finger to his lips, then smiled to himself. "A Winter wren." He showed her its picture. "It's this big." He held his thumb and index finger about four inches apart. *Tiny,* he wrote, **with a big, beautiful song.**

"When I could hear I didn't pay attention to bird songs; now I wish I had."

Jays are noisy, but they can mimic other birds, espe-cially hawks, and there's a secretive little bird called a Wrentit in the forests here that sounds like a ping pong ball bouncing away. Once, on a trip to New Zealand, I heard the dawn chorus of the Bellbirds. They sounded ex-actly like hundreds of bells ringing high in the treetops. That's my favorite memory of a sound. Do you have one?

The note was so long that they stopped in a patch of sunlight while he finished it. Joey looked up at the redwood leaves moving silently against a patch of blue in a slowly graying sky. She thought first of the wind in pines, but when she opened her mouth to answer, that's not what she said. "We always seemed to live near railroad tracks. The places were ugly, but I loved the wail of a train coming. I suppose that isn't a pretty sound to have as a favorite one."

Trains affect a lot of people that way.

She could feel him watching her read. When she handed the pad back, he wrote, *The wail is so lonesome-sounding and the tracks so straight, maybe trains offer a way out of places people don't want to be anymore.*

A chill ran through Joey. She looked at him. "That's it, isn't it? One of the trailers we lived in was the nearest in the park to the tracks. From my room, it seemed like I could see for miles in both directions. I remember wishing Mom and I could slip out one night and just start walking, one way or the other."

Charlie looked at her, thoughtfully, and it seemed as if he wasn't going to let what she'd said end there, but something Sukari was doing got his attention. She sat with her back to them, probing the rotting end of a log with a stick. "What are you doing?" he asked.

Sukari turned and pulled her lips back. A sow bug crawled out from between her teeth and dropped to the ground. Charlie rolled his eyes and shook his head. *She likes how they crunch.*

Joey laughed. "No more kisses for you," she said.

Is there a sound you've never heard that you'd like to? he'd written when she turned again.

"The ocean." Then something else occurred to her: "And my own voice."

He nodded understandingly. "You have a nice voice."

"That's what my mother says, but I must sound funny to people because sometimes they don't understand all of what I say, and I get teased at school. They mimic me by talking through their noses. I can tell by the way their nostrils spread."

Do you go to a speech therapist?

Joey nodded. "On Wednesdays."

Didn't your therapist explain?

"Yeah, but not so I understood. She doesn't like to write to me. She makes me practice reading lips and hers are hard to read."

Charlie shook his head, then walked to Sukari's log and sat down. *Why don't you use hearing aids?*

"They're pretty expensive, and since I haven't quit growing yet, we're waiting to get permanent ones. I have an FM system I use at school. That helps, except I hate wearing the earphones."

You should wear them as often as you can. We learn

words by imitating their sounds. To pronounce new words correctly, you need to hear them and have them spelled phonetically. That's why people miss some of what you say. It's easy to mispronounce new words. My mother never learned to speak. My father tried but no one could understand a thing he said but me. Thank heavens for sign language.

"But hardly any hearing people know sign language, so even if I learned, who would I talk to?"

Charlie grinned and scribbled, *Well, this runt of a chimp and me, for two.*

"That's true. I'm sorry."

He took the pad back and wrote, *How do you do in school?*

"Okay, I guess." Joey shrugged. "I mostly try to get by with lip-reading 'cause I get called bug-head when I wear the head-phones."

We all get teased about something. They called me Twig when I was in school. Hard to believe now. He patted his stomach and smiled. *How well do you communicate with your stepfather and brother?*

Joey shook her head. "Not at all with Ray. He has a long mustache. I brought a sign language book from the library this week, to teach my brother so we could talk, but Mom really wants me to lip-read."

For an instant the expression on Charlie's face reminded her of the fury he'd been in when they first met. "Can you read Luke's lips?" he snapped.

"Well, no, not yet, but then he—"

So you're just supposed to wait until he can speak his words clearly or learns to write? he slashed across the pad.

Joey flinched. She hadn't meant to make him mad. When she took a step back, his expression changed. He shook his head. SORRY, he signed, but he was still mad enough to break the point off his pencil and have to fish for another one before he finished the next note.

If you went to a school for the deaf, you'd get a wonderful education and could go on to college and do just about anything you wanted. Without an education, you will be cut off from making a good life for yourself.

"My friend Roxy is teaching me to sign," she said hopefully.

"Ump. That won't last."

Though Joey knew he was right, still she asked, "How do you know?" Her tone was a little defensive.

"She's thirteen, right?"

"Fourteen."

"She'll get bored."

Joey bit her lip. "I know she will. Her mother's deaf and she's mad at her all the time."

They came out of the pygmy forest onto the hill above her house. Joey put Sukari down. "This is my tree stump, where I come to read, and that's where I live," she told Charlie. "How do I tell Sukari that's my house?"

Charlie signed something, then lifted Sukari onto the stump. Joey put her foot in the springboard hole and boosted herself up to sit beside her. Sukari crossed her legs, folded her arms across her chest, and grinned.

I told her it was new-word time, he wrote. *It's time we give you a sign-name, a short way of referring to you. This is Sukari's sign-name.* Charlie brushed his chin several times with his first two fingers, then wrote, *It means "sweet." Did I tell you her name is Swahili for "sugar"?*

"Yes, sir," Joey said, mimicked the sign, then poked Sukari in the ribs. "That's you," she said.

TICKLE ME, Sukari signed.

NO TICKLE, Charlie said, signing quickly. LATER. NEW WORD.

TICKLE, Sukari signed, standing up and shaking her hands angrily.

NEW WORD. FRIEND NAME, Charlie signed to Sukari, then repeated it for Joey.

Sukari looked at Joey and puckered up, blowing little puffs of sow-bug breath through her long lips. NAME YOU? she signed by placing the first two fingers of one hand over the first two fingers of the other like swords, then pointing a bony finger at Joey.

Joey grinned. MY NAME J-O-E-Y.

VERY GOOD, Charlie signed, said "very," then showed her the sign again. With his little finger he cut a "J" in the air, then added his thumb to make a "Y" just below it. J-Y.

Joey grinned and turned to Sukari. MY NAME J-Y, she signed smoothly.

"Sukari, look," she said, pointing to her house. HOUSE THERE, J-Y. UNDERSTAND?

Sukari looked at Charlie, who repeated the signs for her.

HOUSE YOU, Sukari signed, poking Joey's shoulder before she began to twirl atop the stump, keeping her balance with her knuckles.

When they were back at Charlie's, Sukari let him tie her bib on, then took the spoon full of peanut butter he handed her and climbed into her high chair to eat it.

They'd found chanterelles and Joey stood at the stove, cooking them in butter, green onions, and lots of garlic. She could feel Charlie watching her as he sliced bananas and apples into Sukari's bowl. When he finished, he came to stand beside her, and when she didn't look at him, he tapped her shoulder.

"Why didn't you tell your mother you were coming here today?"

Joey understood enough of what he'd said to answer, but she shrugged instead, then grinned. "I didn't thank you for the letter. That's the first one I've ever gotten."

Charlie smiled. "I used to love to write letters. It will be fun to have an excuse again." He must have thought she'd missed most of what he'd said, because he left and came back with his notepad, on which he'd written, *Do you want to talk about why you didn't tell your mother you were visiting us?*

Joey read what he had written but didn't answer. "These are ready," she said, turning the flame off under the pan. They were having chanterelles and tuna-salad sandwiches, with Oreos for dessert. The early arrival of a drizzly rain had driven their picnic inside.

After they sat down at the table, Joey tried to answer his question: "I didn't tell her I was coming here because I want to learn sign language, and, you know . . . Mom doesn't want me to." She knew that probably wasn't a clear answer but couldn't think of how to explain why one thing was the reason for the other.

Charlie picked up his pencil but wrote only, *The mushrooms are delicious, and it's a treat to have butter. I'm not supposed to have butter or eggs or anything else that tastes good. Bland, fat-free, salt-free, flavor-free food, that's my lot in life.*

"You should have told me," Joey said. "I could have cooked them in water."

"Ugh," Charlie said and made a face, then wrote, *Your mother wants you to fit into the hearing world, but like most hearing people, she doesn't understand the isolation you feel.*

As Joey read what he'd written, she felt the burn of tears and squeezed her eyes shut. He patted her hand and took the pad. *Would you like for me to talk to her?*

"Maybe," Joey said, then changed her mind and shook her head. "I don't think so. It will make her mad that I told you."

Sukari banged her empty Coke can on her high-chair tray for attention, then signed, MORE DRINK.

NO MORE DRINK, Charlie signed, then wrote, *All that sugar makes her hyper.*

Sukari started to scream and bang the can on the tray. Charlie grabbed it away from her. SUKARI BAD, J-Y GO HOME, he signed, but Sukari continued to scream and shake her hands until Joey stood up and began to collect the dishes.

She got quiet. GOOD ME, WASH DISH, she signed.

"She loves to wash dishes," Charlie said, getting up to lift her out of the high chair. When he put her down, she ran across the room and pulled a small step-ladder from the space between the refrigerator and the pantry. Sukari jumped up and down until Charlie opened it and placed it in front of the sink, then she climbed up to sit on the edge.

Charlie ran the sink full so that Sukari could flick the suds with her big toes. She scrubbed and scoured the plastic plates, then rinsed and rinsed them again while Joey waited to dry. "This always takes a while," Charlie said as he put them away.

It had stopped raining by the time they finished. Sukari watched quietly as Joey put her coat on, then went into her room and came back with her little pink plastic coat, one arm already jammed into the wrong sleeve.

"You're not going," Charlie said, taking the coat away from her.

Sukari shrieked and signed, ANGRY, BITE.

"You do and you'll go to jail," Charlie snapped, then scribbled a note to Joey: *Jail is the upside-down playpen in her room. Take your coat off. I'll take her to the bathroom in a minute, then you can make a run for it.*

As soon as Joey took her coat off and returned it to the rack by the door, Sukari grinned, spun, did a somersault, then ran to bring toys from a box in the hall. A moment later she rounded the sofa, pulling a wooden train by a string and carrying poor Hidey like a rag doll.

"Is it potty time?" Charlie asked her, signing "toilet" with a shake of the "T" hand, his thumb jammed between the first two fingers of his fist.

Sukari drew up short and looked at him. J-Y, SUKARI GO TOILET, she signed.

TURTLE, SUKARI GO TOILET, Charlie signed. "You little monster," he said, taking Sukari's hand and leading her down the hall toward the bathroom. Just before he closed the door, he gave a little wave and Joey waved back.

Joey had her coat on and the front door open when Sukari scampered back into the room wearing a toilet-paper stole around her neck. When she saw Joey at the door, she screamed and lunged for her, catching Joey around her legs.

Charlie came around the corner carrying a clean diaper and scolding Sukari, though Joey couldn't tell what he was saying because of the two big safety pins squeezed between his lips. He untied Sukari's arms but she held on tight with her legs.

Charlie caught Sukari's flailing arms in one hand, spit the pins into the palm of his other hand, then put them on the foyer table. He reached down to grab a leg and Joey bent to help him. Sukari let go, but she caught Joey's jacket collar in her little iron fist, and when Joey stood up, the top three buttons popped off and arced away, rolling out of sight beneath various pieces of furniture.

Charlie snatched Sukari up, carried her to her room, shoved her under the upside-down playpen, and set the timer on her dresser.

Sukari grabbed the bars but didn't move.

"Can't she lift that up and get out?"

Charlie nodded. He found his pad and wrote, *She's in it for the raisins. If she stays put for five minutes, she'll get a handful.* "Come on," he said. "I'll move the sofa."

"No, don't worry," Joey said, "I think my mother has one of every button ever made."

No one was home when Joey came in from Charlie's. She took the stairs to her mother and Ray's room three at a time and came back with a needle, thread, and some buttons. She pulled the stool over to use the light above the stove so she could watch the driveway but not be seen herself. One of the buttons was too large and she went to find another. When she came back, Ruth, her arms loaded with groceries, was standing in the kitchen staring at the jacket. She turned to face Joey.

"How did this happen?" she asked, hoisting the bags onto the counter.

"I . . . snagged it on a limb."

Ruth looked at her for a long minute, then said, "Let's see your spore prints."

"I—I didn't do them yet," Joey stammered.

"Where's the homework you did do?"

"In my room."

"Get it," her mother snapped.

Joey knew she was sunk, but she dug the hole deeper. "It was just reading. There's no actual written stuff."

Her mother's eyes narrowed, then she jerked open the drawer beneath the phone and got out the directory. She opened it, flipped some pages, then ran her finger down a column. Before she dialed, she turned so Joey could see her mouth. "Mansell, right?"

Joey didn't answer. Her heart pounded as her mother's fingers jabbed the numbers. When Charlie answered, Ruth turned her back so Joey couldn't see what she said, but she saw her mother grow tense and her hold on the receiver tighten. She hung up and turned around. "A chimpanzee?"

Chapter Five

"She's a baby," Joey said. "She's not dangerous or anything."

She could prove it; the Polaroid was in her jacket pocket, but she was afraid to show it to her mother. Afraid she'd tear it up. When they moved to this house and unpacked the few things they'd brought from Reno, all the pictures of her father had been torn from the album.

Her mother stopped putting cans of soup in the pantry and turned. "You're no judge of that," she said. "She attacked you and ripped your coat."

"Ripping my coat was an accident."

"Stop arguing with me. Don't go over there again. That's final."

Joey ran to her room and slammed the door, then remembered the picture in her jacket. She went back to the kitchen and took her jacket off the stool. Her mother caught her by the shoulder before she reached her room again. "Give that to me. I want to wash it. That monkey's been all over it."

"She's not a monkey. Chimpanzees are apes. Great apes."

She'd read all about them in the library at school. "Our closest relatives."

"Give me the jacket." Her mother held her hand out.

"I need to check the pockets."

"Do it then," she said and went out to bring in more groceries.

Joey slipped the picture from her pocket, slung the coat onto the nearest chair, and slammed into her room again.

An hour later, her mother came into her bedroom and stood with her arms folded until Joey looked up. "We're going to take Luke to see the new Disney movie," she said. "There's stew on the stove, when you get hungry."

Joey nodded and went back to reading.

Her mother didn't move and Joey forced herself not to look up until her mother came and sat on the edge of the bed. "What was in your jacket?"

"Nothing."

"Was it a picture?"

Joey wondered how she knew some of the things she knew. "Yes," she answered.

"May I see it?"

"What for?"

"Is it of the chimpanzee?"

"Yes."

Her mother shrugged. "I just want to see it."

"She's not an it. Her name's Sukari."

" 'It' referred to the picture, not the monk . . . the ape."

"You won't tear it up or anything?"

"Why would I do that?"

Joey shrugged, then reached into the drawer in her nightstand, took the picture out from between two folded sheets of notebook paper, and handed it to her mother.

"It lives in the house?"

Joey nodded, afraid to say anything.

"She's cute." Ruth handed back the picture. "I'm sorry I yelled at you."

"Did you?" Joey tried to smile.

Her mother gave a short snort of a laugh. "Sometimes I forget you can't hear me."

"I still hear your phantom voice, you know, but the tone never changes."

"Do you understand why I don't want you going over to that man's house?"

"Not really. I told you he's old and really nice."

"Joey, you don't have the experience to judge people. Look at Roxy."

"She didn't know that you didn't want me signing."

"She's trash, Joey."

"She's my friend."

"I don't want to hear anything more about her or this old man and his monkey. Is that clear?"

"Totally." Joey had listened to all of this she could stand. She crossed her arms over her chest and closed her eyes. The room fell silent. But the longer she waited, the worse the knot in her stomach got. When the pressure in her ears suddenly changed, she knew her mother had opened the door, but she waited until the shock wave of the door slamming passed through the wall and her headboard to her back before she relaxed and opened her eyes.

As soon as they left for the movie, Joey went and got the phone directory. She dialed Charlie's number, then started to count aloud to ten so that if he picked up, he'd hear her voice. But before she reached ten, she felt the sting of tears. "Charlie, this is Joey Willis," she said, regaining control. "My mom says I can't come over anymore. She says Sukari might be dangerous, but that's not the real reason. I'm not sure what it is but it's not Sukari. I showed her the picture. She's so little in the picture. Charlie, please come talk to my mother. No one understands me like you do. I've never had anyone to talk to before." She paused for a second, trying to think of what else to say. "I had a nice time today."

Sunday morning came and went with no word from Charlie. By midday Joey was sure he hadn't gotten her message, that she'd talked over a phone ringing in an empty house.

To pass the time, she straightened things, made the stack of magazines on the coffee table neater, and collected the newspapers from the last few days, folded them, and put them with the kindling. She used the little dustpan to sweep up around the woodstove. Her mother thanked her, but suspiciously, since it was not Joey's habit to keep house.

Eventually, she took a seat on the sofa opposite Ray's chair and stared up the driveway. Under her breath, she hummed a mantra—*please come*—over and over, rocking a little to the beat.

Ray was watching football. During a commercial he glanced at her and smiled. Twice he'd gone to the kitchen for a beer, stopping to massage her mother's shoulders as she cooked Sunday dinner. While the commercial lasted, they talked with Ruth's back to Joey, so she couldn't see even her mother's half of the conversation. Luke was down for his nap. Joey finally took her jacket from the hall closet and got the book she'd been reading.

Her mother caught the door before Joey could close it behind her. "Where are you going?"

"Out to read," Joey said, holding the book up.

"Why don't you read in here?"

"I'm not going to his house." Joey whirled and ran across the yard, in the opposite direction from her tree stump and the trail to Charlie's.

She glanced back. Her mother stood in the doorway, watching, hands on her hips. Joey kept going, over and down the embankment. Out of sight of her mother, she followed the trail along the creek that curved to flow behind their house, then straightened to cascade past Charlie's on its way to the ocean. When she could see her tree, she began to climb toward it, through the sword ferns and elderberries. Before crossing the back trail, she hid behind an alder and peeked to make sure her mother wasn't watching from the kitchen window, then she darted across and up the steep incline to her stump.

The little tarp was heavy when she pulled it out and her first thought was that it had somehow filled with rainwater, but when she picked it up by a corner, a package fell out: a wrapped package, with silver paper and a blue bow. For a moment, she thought it was a gift for someone else, mistakenly left in her hiding place, but the envelope stuck beneath the ribbon had "Joey Willis" written on it in Charlie's shaky handwriting. She turned it over to open. On the back he'd scrawled, *I'm too old. It was Sukari who remembered how to find this tree.*

Joey spread the tarp across the top of the stump, folding an edge over so as not to smother the red huckleberry sprout that had taken root in the tree's rotting core.

The long letter started with "Dear Jo y." The "e" was missing, cut out with a hole punch, leaving a small, empty circle.

I had such a nice time today, and so did Sukari. She adores you, and why not—you're much more fun than a slow old man. I think she's found a soul-mate.

I decided I'd write and tell you more about my parents and what my life was like growing up. Hearing you speak of your friend Roxy reminded me how angry I used to get at my parents, and the burden I thought they were because they didn't talk or read lips. I, like Roxy, was their bridge. That's a huge responsibility for a kid.

My mother was born deaf and never heard a single word, she never spoke, though oddly she had a wonderful laugh that I still miss. When she was young, the traditional thinking was to make the deaf learn to speak, but luckily, her parents quickly gave up that notion. They wanted to be able to communicate with her themselves so they sent her to a school that taught American Sign Language and they learned it, too.

My father was a baby, just learning to talk, when he lost his hearing. His parents were caught up in the same debate, but they chose the other path. It was a terrible handicap. Because it took so long to teach him to approximate the sound of each word, the rest of his education had to wait. What little speech he learned, no one could understand. The frustration finally drove him to quit school in the eighth grade and take the only job he could find—a janitor. The good news is that the job was at a school for the deaf. That's where he met my mother and where he learned to sign. Eventually, he found his life's work as a printing press operator (the perfect fit for him; presses make a "deafening" racket). He made a good living and they were happy. We were happy.

Don't get me wrong. Both arguments have valid points. But if I had to decide for a child of mine, I would choose sign language. If we hadn't all signed, I would not have been able to talk to my own parents.

I just got the call from your mother. I'm sorry she was upset. I had to tell her that Sukari ripped your jacket because I think she thought I did it. I think I should come by and meet your parents and maybe bring Sukari. She'd love Luke. Just her size and speed. But I'll wait for your okay. I don't want to make things worse.

This is a little gift to you from me and the runt. I hope with time, it opens a new world for you.

Love,
C and S

Cautiously, so as not to ruin the beautiful paper, Joey undid
the bow and eased the tape loose. It was a book: *The Joy of
Signing*. Between the "o" and the "y" in Joy, Charlie had pasted
the "e" he'd cut out of her name, making the new title *The Jo^{e}y
of Signing*. Inside the front cover he'd written, **To Joey Willis,
remember all you are unable to do is hear. Love from your
friends—Charlie and Sukari.** Sukari had scribbled her signature, too.

Joey bit her lip, but it didn't work. She covered the little "e"
with her index finger, hugged the book, and sobbed.

After she'd cried herself out, she spent the next hour signing all the words in the first chapter, "Family Relationships,"
then practiced a sentence, nearly each word of which she had
to look up. THANK-YOU FOR THE SIGN LANGUAGE
BOOK, she signed over and over to herself.

When she got cold, she drew up her legs and covered herself
with an edge of the tarp, and worked on signing, MY NAME IS
J-O-E-Y W-I-L-L-I-S. WHAT IS YOUR NAME?

She stayed gone a couple of hours. When she came down the
hill from her tree, her mind was still busy tracing the shapes
that words took on the hands. She passed the kitchen window as
she came along the rear walkway and saw her mother ironing
with hard, fast strokes. Ruth glanced up, stony-faced, as she
passed. Joey wondered if her mother knew she'd been signing
and was taking her anger out on Ray's shirt. She believed her
mother had the freakish ability to know what she was up to all
the time. As much as she wanted this to change since meeting
Charlie and Sukari, Joey accepted it as a price she paid for the
ease with which they communicated. She read her mother's

lips and moods and in exchange her mother read her secret thoughts. Though she'd left the book wrapped in the tarp, Joey believed that hiding places—tree hollows or the heart—were no barriers to her mother's second sight. She was at the front door before she saw Charlie's car in the driveway.

Charlie was talking and watching football with Ray, who had Luke on his lap.

"Hi," Charlie said. "I thought it was time for us to meet your family." He winked, took a notepad from his shirt pocket, and handed it to her. He'd already written, *I got your message. It was on the answering machine when I got back from leaving your present. Did you find it?*

Joey nodded and smiled. She felt such relief, she wanted to hug him.

"Where's Sukari?"

Charlie jerked his thumb toward his car.

"Luke," Joey said. "Want to meet a chimpanzee?"

Charlie tapped Joey's shoulder. "Your mother."

Joey turned.

"No. She might bite him."

"I want to see the chimpagnee," Luke shouted.

Joey was facing her mother, so she didn't see what was said next, but her mother leveled her icy stare at Ray and said, "If it hurts him, I'll . . . I'll never forgive you."

"I'll bring Sukari in here. They can play in Luke's room."

"I don't want that animal in the—" Ruth stopped and glared at Joey. "Fleas," she said, then returned to punishing the ironing.

"Come on, Luke." Joey held out her hand.

Sukari was stretched out on the ledge behind the backseat with a magazine. I-SEE-YOU, J-Y.

"Did you see that, Luke? She talks with her hands." Joey opened the door.

Luke scooted behind Joey's legs and peeked around as Sukari rolled off the ledge and dropped onto the backseat, stood, and wobbled toward them. NAME BOY? Sukari asked.

"His name is Luke. L-U-K-E. He came to play with you."

Sukari clearly understood the word "play" because she grinned and signed, TICKLE-CHASE, by slapping the back of her hand with her index finger.

"She said she wants to play chase," Joey told Luke.

Luke held tightly to Joey's leg and shook his head.

Joey scooped Sukari into her arms, kissed her, then took Luke's hand and led him to a lawn chair. "Would you like Sukari to teach you to talk with your hands?"

Luke shook his head no.

"Well, let's learn one word, okay?" FRIEND, Joey signed. "Luke and Sukari." FRIEND FRIEND.

Sukari hooked her index fingers, then poked Luke's shoulder.

Luke hooked his fingers and poked Sukari.

CHASE, Sukari signed.

"She wants the Bear to chase her."

Luke made claws and a snarly-face.

"Oops," Joey said and glanced at Sukari for her reaction to Luke's teeth. "Don't scare her, okay?"

Sukari seemed oblivious. She signed, CHASE ME, BOY.

Joey interpreted.

Luke giggled, jumped off Joey's lap, and ran at Sukari. Sukari loped away on bowed legs and knuckles, slowed a bit for him to catch up, then launched herself up an alder tree and dangled by one hand from a branch just above his head.

Luke looked stunned for a second. "Come here, monkey," he snapped.

Sukari swung to another limb and then another until she'd gone all the way up the trunk and was back where she'd begun.

"Do this, Luke." Joey made Sukari's chase-sign.

CHASE, Luke signed, then flung his elbows up and charged across the yard with Sukari on his heels. He shrieked when Sukari caught him and rolled with him on the ground. Joey glanced at the house to see if the rough-housing would bring her mother running.

Ruth stood at the kitchen window with her arms folded across her chest. Joey signaled, OKAY. Her mother nodded. *You just read your first sign, Mom,* she thought, then turned away so her mother wouldn't see her grin.

Sukari had raced off and climbed up the rungs on the power pole.

Luke formed a gun with his index finger and thumb and rushed forward, screaming "pow, pow, pow."

Sukari climbed higher. Too high. "Come down, Sukari," Joey said, shushing Luke. "Come down." CHASE BOY.

The bottom rung was about six feet off the ground. When Sukari's foot touched it she launched herself at Joey, who caught her and swung her around and around by her arms.

"Do me. Do me," Luke shouted.

While Joey swung Luke, Sukari flailed her arms for another turn, so she made them link hands, and, holding their free hands, swung them both. When she put them down, Luke signed, CHASE, and ran with Sukari on his heels. When he turned to see if Sukari was gaining on him, Joey shouted a warning, but he hit the power pole full-bore. He fell to the ground, shrieking and holding his head. Sukari squatted beside him and touched the bump, then turned to Joey and signed, BOY HURT. HUG BOY. She wrapped her long arms around Luke, patted his back, and kissed him. Luke sniffled, then grinned.

Sukari looked up and signed something Joey couldn't interpret. At the same moment Ruth ran up, arms swinging as if she was going to pummel Sukari. "Get away from him," she screamed.

Sukari screamed, too, fell backward, then scampered away and back up the power pole. "Where did she bite you?" Ruth cried, inspecting Luke's arms, then his legs. "Oh my God." She tilted his head and inspected the red welt on his forehead.

"Mom, she didn't bite him. He ran into the pole. Sukari was comforting him."

Luke jerked on Joey's pants leg. "I want to hug the monkey," he shouted. His bottom lip jutted and quivered threateningly.

"Well, ask her to hug you." Joey knelt down, hesitated, then showed Luke the signs.

"Monkey," he said. WANT HUG.

"She uses sign language?" Ruth asked.

Joey nodded, expecting her mother to sneer.

GIRL MAD, Sukari signed, pointing at Ruth. BITE SUKARI.

"She won't bite you." Joey glanced at her mother. "She thinks you're going to bite her. You won't, will you?" She grinned.

"It's not funny. They're playing too rough and I don't want her licking him in the face," Ruth said.

"She's not a dog, Mom. She was kissing Luke's boo-boo. Right?" She mussed his hair.

WANT HUG, Luke signed.

Sukari came down slowly but stayed on the bottom rung, just out of reach.

"Mommy, go 'way," Luke said.

Sukari watched Ruth walk slowly back to the house. When she was far enough away, Sukari hooted, swung down, and ran on bowlegs and knuckles into Luke's outstretched arms, bowling him over with kisses.

At the front door, her mother stopped to watch. In the instant before she went inside and closed the door, Joey thought she saw her smile.

It began to get chilly after the sun slipped behind the trees, but when Joey came to the door with Luke and Sukari, her mother waved for her attention. "They're all dirty; keep them outside." She tossed Joey a damp dishtowel.

Charlie stood up. "I guess we'd better be going," he said, lifting Sukari off Joey's shoulders.

"No," Luke howled. "I want the monkey to stay."

Charlie flinched. "She's not a monkey, son, she's an ape."

"I want the ape to stay," Luke wailed.

Sukari squirmed and leaned toward Joey, signing, HUG, HUG.

"I'll take them back outside," she said. "You stay. Please. I want you to get to know each other. Charlie's parents were deaf," she told Ray.

Ray's brow furrowed and he said something to Charlie under his mustache.

Charlie patted Ray's shoulder and said something that Joey couldn't see because he was turned so she couldn't see his mouth. Whatever it was, Ray glanced at Joey, his always sad eyes sadder.

Joey avoided looking at her mother. She took Sukari back from Charlie and kissed her. "Come on, Bear," she said to Luke, who burst out the door ahead of her.

Charlie picked up his empty beer can and shook it. "Sure, I'd love another."

It had gotten quite cold when Luke jerked on Joey's sleeve and pointed to the front door. Charlie and her parents were on the front deck. Her mother motioned for them to come. She no longer looked mad, but she wasn't happy, either.

Sukari, who was wearing Luke's cowboy boots, signed, NO GO, when she saw Charlie, then took off running toward the woods. The boots, which were on the wrong feet, tripped her up. Joey tackled her as she tried to scramble away and carried her screaming to the car, where Charlie strapped her into her car seat.

SUKARI MAD. BITE, she signed.

Whatever Charlie said to her had a sobering effect. Sukari hugged herself and blew angry little puffs of air through her long lips.

Charlie turned from scolding Sukari to shake hands with Ray, then with Luke, then Ruth, who paused before smiling stiffly and taking his hand. When he came to Joey, she hesitated a moment, then hugged him quickly. THANK-YOU. SIGN LANGUAGE BOOK, she signed.

Ruth reached to stop Joey, but Ray caught her mother's wrist in midair. Ruth jerked it free and jammed her hand into her apron pocket.

Chapter Six

The second Charlie was out of sight, Ruth grabbed Joey's arm and spun her around. "You told him, didn't you?"

Joey's heart leapt and she threw her arm up to block the blow she expected.

It was her mother who looked as if she'd been slapped. She let go. "I've never hit you."

"Your grabbing scared me."

"Sorry," she said, "but you did tell him, didn't you?"

Joey shook her head.

"Why would you tell a complete stranger our secrets?"

"I didn't tell him," Joey cried and tried to turn away.

Her mother tightened her grip on Joey's arm. "I'm not through talking to you."

Ray suddenly stepped between them, breaking Ruth's hold. He must have said something in defense of Charlie, because her mother snapped, "How would you know? Someone to watch football and drink beer with is not a measure of the man." With that she spun on her heels and, dragging Luke, marched into the house.

Her stepfather turned, gave Joey's shoulder a squeeze, then followed her mother. The argument continued. Joey slipped in and began to set the table for dinner. She caught only the parts her mother wanted her to see or a snatch here and there when Ruth faced Ray directly, often shaking a spatula to emphasize a point: "---------- stranger butting ---------- our -------
--- pushing her to learn sign language."

Ruth glanced at her then deliberately—so that Joey could see every word—and said, "You want her to use a language a monkey can learn. Sign language." She snorted. "It's a contradiction in terms." She shook a finger at Joey. "No signing. I won't allow it."

Joey's hands began to tremble. She put the plates on the table before she dropped them. *I knew this would happen.* Ray looked at her and shook his head, warning her off going further with this, but she couldn't let that be the last word. "Stop calling her a monkey," she shouted. "She's a chimpanzee. And signing lets us know how she feels, what she's thinking, and what she wants. That's more than I can tell about my own brother." She ran to her room, slammed and locked her door.

The Old Dock Café was opening early Monday to host a breakfast for some group or other. Since her mother had to be there to help set up, she insisted on taking Joey to school, as if not letting her ride the bus was a form of punishment.

Ruth pulled up in front of the middle school. Smoke from her cigarette formed a gray haze in the closed car. Joey put her hand on the door handle and glanced at her mother, who continued to stare straight ahead. Ruth hadn't spoken to her since last night.

Joey opened the car door and stepped out but held on to the handle. Her heart hammered as it always did when she had something she wanted to say. Speaking up for herself terrified her but her mother's silence was crushing. Before she met Charlie and Sukari, only the sight of her mother's lips moving made her feel a part of things. When her mother punished her, turning so Joey couldn't see what she said to Luke or to Ray, it was as if a lid had been clamped down on the jar she lived in, and twisted shut, airtight. Now Joey stood gripping the door, holding her mother in place. Her breath came in short gasps the way it did after a good cry. "He understands what it's like for me," she said.

Her mother, without looking at her, reached across, pulled the door closed, and drove away.

Joey bit her lip to keep from crying. It wasn't until she turned that she saw Kenny watching from the front steps. He didn't smile or wave; he turned, as Joey did, to watch Ruth pull into the Senior Center parking lot, make a U-turn, and head back the way they'd come.

"I didn't tell him," Joey whispered, as she passed without looking over.

Kenny was at her favorite table when she came into biology class. He had a foot on one of the chairs. When Joey hesitated, he dropped it to the floor and motioned for her to come over. He'd been doodling on a piece of notebook paper: *No Fear,* with jagged lightning bolts and a very good pirate's face with angular cheekbones, square jaw, and a patch over one eye. He flipped the page to expose a clean sheet when she sat down. *Hi,* he wrote.

Joey almost laughed, but she was too touched. "Hi," she said.

Last week's notes, he wrote, then handed her photocopies of the notes he'd scribbled in class. At the top he'd written *For Joey.* The "o" in her name was a tiny heart.

She blinked, sure her imagination had created it out of sloppy handwriting, but it was there. "Thank you." She quickly put them away as if she hadn't noticed.

How was your weekend?

"Good. Yours?"

Same ole. Your old lady looked mad this morning.

"She was."

How come?

Joey shrugged.

Kristin and Jason came in, trying to elbow each other aside to be the first to reach the table. Out of the corner of her eye, Joey saw Kenny cover what he'd written with his drawings.

Jason won and fell into the chair with his back to the teacher. "What's happening?"

Before she could answer, she saw Kristin glance at the ceiling. "Nothing much," Joey mouthed.

"Gotcha, dork." Kenny laughed and high-fived Joey, who blushed with pleasure.

In math, which was her best subject, there was a test, so time flew. She turned her paper in the minute she was done and left to get to the cafeteria ahead of the crowd.

Motion was sound. Joey heard with her eyes, so the running, pushing, shoving, arm-waving, ball-and-book tossing, the scrape of chairs and tables in the cafeteria, in the mood she was in, was more noise than her eyes could stand. Brad was at a back table, waiting for Roxy, but Joey didn't want to be with them. She got a sandwich and took it to eat at her favorite spot behind the library where trees grew densely on a steep hillside. There was a high chain-link fence along the property line, which kept her from actually finding a good spot in the woods. But between the driveway along the rear of the building and the fence was a line of trees and one stump. Her stump. Before she met Roxy, she used to go there every day and sit with her back against the fence and read while she ate.

As she was leaving the cafeteria with her lunch, she caught a glimpse of Kenny paying for his. He was with a couple of friends and either hadn't seen her or pretended he hadn't. She scooted out quickly before he caught her looking. She was afraid to let how he'd acted in biology class mean too much.

She sat with her book on her knees; the second half of her sandwich kept the pages from flipping. She hadn't seen Kenny coming and nearly jumped out of her skin when he kicked her foot, tipping the book off her knee and dropping her sandwich onto the ground.

"Sorry," he said and bent to pick them up.

"No problem. I was full." She took her sandwich, turned and jammed it through the fence for a possum or raccoon to get later.

He handed her a sheet of notebook paper. *How come you eat out here by yourself?*

Joey shrugged. "I like it here."

Kenny squatted to sit on his haunches. "Can you read lips?"

"Sometimes. Some people's lips are easier to read than others."

"Are mine easy or hard?"

"Medium." She smiled.

"I dried two ----------" He glanced away. "---------- wood bee ----------." He looked down to open a bag of chips. "---------- deaf ----------." He offered her some as he chewed. "---------- mug my ----------." He wiped his mouth on the back of his hand. "---------- enough not to hear."

Joey couldn't even attempt a bluff. She shook her head. "Sorry, I missed too much of that."

Kenny balanced his notebook on his knee and wrote, *I tried to imagine what it would be like to be deaf but I couldn't plug my ears enough not to hear. What is it like?*

"Real quiet."

Kenny's serious, sympathetic expression lit up at her answer, then he laughed. "Like, duh."

In spite of trying to stay calm and cool, Joey blushed again, hating herself for not being able to keep her color under control. "That's okay. It's a good question. I wasn't always deaf so I know the difference and that's pretty much it. There are no sounds except really loud noises like motorcycles and car horns, chain saws, stuff like that. All the pretty sounds are gone. Like I've never heard the ocean."

It sounds whooshy.

Joey grinned. "That's the best description I've ever seen."

"Are the scars where . . ." He reached and lightly brushed aside her hair. "They tried to fix your hearing?"

The question caught Joey off guard. She kept her hair medium length and bushy to cover those scars. No one had ever seemed to notice them before. Without thinking, she touched the one behind her right ear. "Not . . . Well, yes. Sort of."

To her relief, he was writing his next question: *Do you and your parents talk in sign language?*

"That's what my mother was mad about." Joey hesitated. She wanted to tell him everything, especially about Sukari.

What do you mean?

"My mother doesn't want me to learn sign language."

"How come?"

Her mother's face popped into her mind. "Dumb reasons," Joey said, deciding it was better not to go where the details would lead. "Have you ever heard about Washoe, the chimpanzee who uses sign language? I read all about her in a *National Geographic*."

"I thought . . ." he said, then wrote it instead: *I thought it was a gorilla.*

"Koko is the gorilla who signs, but Washoe was the first and she's a chimpanzee. She's still alive, I think. Someplace."

What about her?

"I know a chimpanzee that signs. My neighbor owns her and I bet he'd let you meet her if you wanted to."

Kenny's head bobbed. "Rad."

"What?"

Radical. Cool.

"Oh." Joey nodded. "Her name is Sukari. . . ."

"What?"

"The chimp. Her name is Sukari. That's Swahili for 'sugar.' She's just a baby, but you can talk to her with your hands. I know the alphabet and a few words. I'm teaching myself with the sign language book her owner gave me and I could show you a few . . ."

He glanced away.

". . . words. . . ." Her voice trailed off.

"Yeah. Sure." Kenny stood up. "There's the bell." He held his hand out to help her up. "Want to eat together tomorrow?"

Joey nodded and took his hand but felt she could have just as easily floated to her feet.

On Tuesday, Joey waited in the library for Roxy, but she never showed up, nor was she in the cafeteria when she got her sandwich and went to meet Kenny. She was disappointed. She wanted to tell her about Kenny and hoped they could all sit together at lunch now that she kind of had a boyfriend, too.

Roxy wasn't in class on Wednesday, either. On Thursday, Joey saw her sitting alone with Brad in the far corner of the cafeteria. They both looked upset and Joey guessed they were having an argument.

Joey got to history class early, running through the rain, to make sure she was there early enough to save Roxy a seat beside her. Each time the pressure in her ears changed with the opening of the door, she looked up. When the door opened and it was Roxy, she looked as if she'd been crying.

Maybe it's rain, Joey thought. She smiled and moved her backpack off the seat of the desk next to hers.

Roxy glanced her way, then walked to the back of the room and flopped into a desk in the last row.

Joey waved for her attention. "I saved this for you," she mouthed.

Roxy looked away.

Joey felt the sting of tears, blinked them back, and turned around.

After class, she caught up with Roxy, who had fled the room the second the bell rang. "What's the matter?" Joey asked, catching her sleeve.

Roxy pulled away. "Nothing."

"Why were you crying?"

"Me? Don't be ridiculous."

"Are you mad"—Joey lowered her voice when other kids slowed to look at them—"at me?"

Roxy stopped and turned to face her. "Read my lips. Leave me alone."

Joey felt as if she'd been slapped. Roxy spun, marched a few feet, then turned again. "I'm sick to death of deaf people," she shouted.

Joey couldn't move. She stood like a rock in a stream, holding her stomach and staring at Roxy's back. It wasn't until someone took her arm and led her out under the breezeway that she felt the cold air on her wet cheeks and knew she'd been crying. She looked up. Kenny smiled at her and wiped a tear away with his thumb.

"I don't know what I did to make her hate me," Joey said.

"It's not you. Understand?"

Joey nodded.

Kenny opened his notebook to a blank page, held it against the wall, and wrote, *It's crap with her mother.*

Joey watched for him to write more. When he didn't, she looked up.

"Like what?"

I don't know exactly, but Dillon said, her old lady is getting back together with her father, who's a real piece of work, and they are moving away.

"She just moved here."

Kenny nodded. "I know. That's why she's so upset. Her mother's DEAF, right?"

Joey blinked. "You signed."

I kinda looked up a few words. You want to go to Goodings for a Coke or something?

Joey was almost too moved to speak. "I . . . I can't really," she said finally. "I have to catch the bus."

Kenny shrugged. "I live in town. My brother could take you home later. Understand?"

"Yes, I do. This is the sign for understand." She flicked her index finger away from her forehead.

"Cool."

They walked, without trying to talk, down Franklin Street toward Goodings, the hamburger and malt shop on the corner opposite the post office. The sleeves of their jackets brushed against each other as they walked and it felt electric. *Is this like my first date?* she wondered, then decided it was close enough. That's what she'd tell Charlie when she saw him this weekend.

She thought about Roxy as they walked and wished she could have told her that she understood. Her mother had gone back to her father a bunch of times. Still, Joey guessed it wouldn't have helped Roxy to know that, not while they were still at the mercy of their parents.

The days got longer, the daffodils bloomed, and the rusty-sided Allen's hummingbirds returned to engage the year-round Anna's hummingbirds in warfare over possession of the feeders.

Joey felt the same tug. Though her mother never said another word one way or the other about her visits to see Charlie and Sukari, Joey never said that was where she was going. Instead, she took a book, and told Ruth she was going out to read. Only if it rained did she stay home to keep up the pretense.

She'd slipped *The Joy of Signing* into the house and hidden it under the blankets and afghans in the cedar chest at the foot of her bed. Now, whenever she was home alone, she practiced signing.

One day, she was sitting on the side of her bed facing the window, practicing "Location and Direction," when she looked up and saw her mother's reflection in the glass of her sliding door. Her hands froze. Neither of them moved, then Joey slowly turned around. Her mother just stared at her. Joey's heart thudded in her chest.

A small washer-dryer unit, one on top of the other, was in a little closet in Joey's room. Her mother held a load of dirty clothes. "As long as you're not sneaking over to that old man's house today," she said, "you can wash these." She dropped the whole load on the floor. She stopped in the hallway and looked back at Joey before grabbing the knob and slamming the door.

Joey took a deep breath. *She's known all along,* she thought. *Why did she wait till now to get mad?* Then Joey realized something about her mother, and about herself, that she should have seen before. They were still afraid of conflict—her mother more so than herself. Ruth let irritations fester even though it was now safe to get angry. Recognizing this suddenly made Joey feel older. She thought about Roxy, whom she'd never seen again, and realized that her fury that day was Roxy toughing it out, trying to cope with her frustration at being uprooted on a parental impulse. As Joey sorted the pile of laundry into darks and lights, she knew that she was free to continue teaching herself to sign. *Mom just threw in the towel,* she thought, dropping one into the washer.

That Saturday dawned sunny and warm. Joey was on the stool at the kitchen counter eating a waffle when her mother came running from the bathroom, her hair wrapped in a towel, and grabbed the receiver.

Her expression soured immediately after she said hello, and she turned her back. When she hung up, she looked at Joey. "That was your *friend*. He wants you to go to Pine Beach with him and the chimp for a picnic."

Joey's eyes lit up, then clouded just as quickly. "What did you tell him?"

"I told him you could go."

Joey jumped off the stool and hugged her mother. "Thank

you. Thank you," she cried, started for her room, then came back. WHAT TIME? she signed before she caught herself and clamped her hands into fists. "What time?" she asked.

Her mother had watched Joey draw her right index finger across the upturned fingers of her left hand, then point at her watch dial. She looked up. "It's bad enough you are learning that . . . that *language* against my will. Don't use it in this house," she snapped.

Joey flinched. "I forgot."

"Damn that old man."

"It's not his fault."

"Whose fault is it then that you're going against my wishes and learning to talk with your hands like a mute?"

The madder her mother got, the faster she talked, the harder it was to read her lips. Joey missed some of what she'd said. "I want to . . ." she said, then lost her nerve.

"You want to what?"

Her insides trembled. She wanted to shout, *I'm sick of only having you to talk to. I hate my nasal-sounding voice. Charlie says I have pretty hands to speak with. Poetry in motion, he said.* But she hooked her bottom lip with her teeth and clenched and un-clenched her fists. "Nothing," she said.

Ruth stared at her for a moment, eyes narrowed, then she nodded and turned to go back to the bathroom, fluffing her wet hair with the towel.

Joey almost let it end there. Almost. "People make faces when I talk," she said so softly that she didn't think she'd spoken out loud.

But her mother turned. "We'll get you more therapy."

"If I can't read somebody's lips, they don't bother trying to talk to me."

"You think talking with your hands will change that? You should practice reading lips instead."

"I do, but why can't I do both?"

"Well you are, aren't you?"

"Yeah, but in secret, like it was against the law or something. Why can't I teach it to Luke and to Ray so I could talk to them?"

"I don't understand this, Joey. You can talk to them now."

"But, Mom, they can't talk to me. I can't read their lips or very many other people's. I don't hold conversations with anyone but you, and Charlie because he writes his half."

"Well, practice more. If you get better at reading lips you can talk to everybody in the world and nobody has to learn that stunted language."

"You think because I can read your lips I should be able to read anybody's. Watch TV without the sound on, Mom. See how hard it is and how different people talk. Some lips are impossible, like Ray's because of his mustache and other people who hardly move their mouths when they talk. It's not that easy. You try it." Joey realized she was shouting and looked down.

"I don't want to argue this with you again. Sign language is not the answer. Use it to talk to that chimp if you want to, but don't use it in public. People will feel sorry for you. You don't want to encourage pity, do you?"

"Charlie says . . ." came out of her mouth before she could stop herself, so she plunged ahead, "it's more pitiful to be left out of everything."

Her mother had been softening but her expression changed swiftly at the mention of Charlie's name. "Well, I'll tell you what," she snapped. "You want to learn sign language so bad, you can stay home today and practice." Her mother turned away.

Sometimes Joey forgot that other people could hear even when their backs were turned. This was one of those moments. "No," she whispered.

Her mother whirled around. "What do you mean, no?"

Joey felt her knees get rubbery. Faces disfigured by anger made her want to run and her knees always threatened to fail her.

"Nothing," she said. She took a step backward, lifted her plate up off the counter, and held it with both hands in front of her stomach. "I want to go to the beach."

"You should have thought of that before you sassed me."

"I'm sorry."

"Well, while you're sitting here today, you can think about how just being sorry isn't always enough."

After her mother went back into the bathroom and closed the door, Joey stood holding her plate for a few minutes, looking down at her reflection in the syrupy slick. She tilted the plate one way then the other, distorting her features, then carried it to the sink to rinse but decided to leave it; maybe her mother would see herself in it, too. She got her coat and left the house.

As soon as she reached the edge of the yard, she glanced over her shoulder, expecting to see her mother coming at her. But there was no one there, just silence, sunlight, and a humming-bird at the feeder. Joey turned and started to run, down the trail toward Charlie's.

Chapter Seven

When she came out of the woods at Charlie's side yard, Joey
saw an unfamiliar car in his driveway and felt like crying. If she
went in, she'd have to cope with trying to read a stranger's lips
or with being ignored, which she preferred.

She leaned against a tree to catch her breath and to try to decide what to do. Go in or go home. *Charlie's expecting me,* she
thought. Her mother had told him she could go to the beach,
though by now she must have called to tell him to send her
home. If she hadn't, Joey could play with Sukari until his guest
left.

She crossed the yard and went up the front steps.

A pretty, blond woman, a bit younger than her mother, answered the door when she knocked. "Are you Joey?" she asked
slowly, though with little exaggeration. "I expected a little
girl," she said, drawing the thumb of the "A" hand down her
cheek to her chin, then clipping herself at the waist. "You're
tall, and beautiful."

Joey blushed and ducked her head.

"I'm Lynn." L-Y-N-N. She fingerspelled her name. "Charlie's niece from Fresno."

Joey shook the offered hand. "Is Charlie here?"

"Sure, sure, sorry. Come in." She stood aside.

Joey stepped into the foyer and glanced around. Lynn tapped her shoulder. "They're on the deck," she said, then signed, SORRY, I DON'T KNOW SIGN LANGUAGE. "Well," she said, then grinned, "except the alphabet and how to say 'I don't know sign.' "

Joey liked Lynn instantly, as she often did with people whose lips were easy to read. "That's okay," she said. "I don't know much myself."

From the living room, Joey could see Sukari dangling by one hand from the crossbar of her jungle gym and Charlie in a lounge chair. His eyes were closed, and even in the sun, his skin was the color of concrete.

Joey reached out and caught Lynn's arm. "Is he sick?"

Lynn's brow crinkled, then she shook her head. "Just a little tired, I think."

Sukari spotted Joey, shrieked, dropped to the deck, and scrambled to meet her.

Joey grabbed her up and hugged her. "How's my good girl?" she asked, waving at Charlie, who had jolted upright.

GOOD DEVIL ME, she signed.

"I can't argue with that," Joey said and laughed.

GO J-Y HOUSE, Sukari signed.

NO, STAY YOUR HOUSE.

Sukari rolled her upper lip, then signed, TICKLE-CHASE.

Joey tipped Sukari onto her back, then blew into the fur on her belly. When she lifted her head, Charlie motioned for her to come outside.

Joey leaned and kissed his cheek. "Did Mom call?"

"I don't think so. Did she?" he asked Lynn.

Lynn nodded, then turned to Joey. "She asked if you were here and I said no. But she said if you showed up to send you home. Understand?"

"Yes," Joey said. "We had a fight," she said to Charlie. "I accidentally signed in front of her."

"This has got to stop," he said to Lynn, but Joey read his lips.

Though it was quite chilly, even in the sun, Charlie's forehead and upper lip beaded with perspiration.

His niece patted his arm. "Don't get upset. Doctor's orders."

"Somebody has got to fight this battle for her," Charlie snapped.

Joey's eyes flicked from mouth to mouth trying to keep up. "Doctor?" she said.

Lynn turned and smiled. "My orders. I'm a doctor. Understand?"

"Quit asking her if she understands," Charlie scolded. "This means 'understand.' " He flicked his finger off his forehead. "And this is doctor," he added, putting the "D" hand against the pulse in his wrist. "Where's my notepad?" he demanded.

"Grouch," Lynn muttered and winked at Joey.

Charlie took the pad Lynn handed him. *She shows up every month to check on me and the nursemaid in her comes out.*

"You need a nursemaid," Lynn said, then pointed to what she'd written at the bottom of the pad: *I'm an obstetrician: I deliver babies.* As Joey read, she leaned over her shoulder and added, *He's more trouble than ten babies.*

Joey smiled, but there was something about the way Charlie looked that worried her. "Are you sure you're okay?"

Her hovering is enough to make you think you're sick.

Lynn jumped up and ran into the house. When she came back, she looked peeved, and gave Joey a thin-lipped smile. "That was your mother again." She took the pad and wrote, *I think you'd better go home. She sounded pretty mad.*

Joey tried to smile. "I forgot she wanted me to babysit," she said, because she didn't want to upset Charlie any more than he was.

He frowned and crossed his arms over his chest. "Was that before or after she said you could go to the beach?"

Joey shrugged.

Sukari, who'd been sitting in another chair with her animal-alphabet book, quietly signing to her doll and to Hidey, stuck her bottom lip out and crossed her arms.

SEE-YOU LATER, Joey signed, then grinned and said, "I'm getting good."

NO GO, CHASE SUKARI. She deserted the kitten and the doll, ran across the deck, and scrambled up the drainpipe.

Charlie held the pad up: *You'd better make a run for it.*

Joey nodded.

Sukari was perched on the eave. CHASE-ME.

LATER. J-Y TOILET, she signed, then slipped into the house,

turning to wave when she reached the door. Lynn was holding a screaming chimp.

She signed I-LOVE-YOU and ducked out.

Joey dragged out the walk home, hoping that if she stalled long enough Ray would be there. Since her parents had argued over her signing, her mother had avoided confronting Joey when Ray was around.

But Ray wasn't home. Ruth met her at the door, drying her hands on a dishtowel. "I said no beach."

"I didn't go to the beach."

"I told you to stay here. You went to that old man's house. You're grounded," her mother snapped.

"Great," Joey said, and started for her room, but stopped and faced her mother. "What does that mean, Mom? That I can't watch TV for a week? No radio? The dance is off?" Her voice began to shake. "I can't be with any of my many friends? What does it mean?" she shouted, then ran into her room and slammed the door. She covered her ears and screamed, "What *does* it mean?"

The door flew open. "You are a different person since you met that old man," her mother said. "I'll tell you what grounded means. You are never to go near that house again. Ever."

Joey lay on her bed, staring at the ceiling. She thought of running away, but that was such a joke, she almost laughed. She'd read about a boy in Florida who divorced his parents. Maybe she could do that. Ask the courts to award her to Charlie. The question of whether or not he'd take her was kicking around in her mind when the door opened as if it had been blown in by a gust of wind. Her mother motioned for her to come.

Joey sat up and wiped her eyes on her sleeves. "What?"

"Just come," her mother snapped.

Charlie and Lynn were in the living room. Charlie sat in Ray's chair; Lynn stood beside him, one hand on his shoulder, the other on her hip.

Charlie looked up when Joey came in and tried to smile. He was bundled up as if it were snowing out, and his skin was still an ashy-gray. "I had to come," he said to Joey. It was an apology.

"I'm glad you did." Joey wanted to hug him and tell him she'd just been wishing he'd rescue her. She smiled at Lynn. "I'm glad you came, too. Did you meet my mother?"

Lynn nodded. "I tried to stop him," she said to Ruth. "I don't think this is his business. She's your daughter."

Joey caught just enough of Lynn's words to feel betrayed.

Charlie brushed Lynn's hand off his shoulder. "Don't undermine me. She needs to understand what this is about and I better do it while I can."

"Charlie, not today," Joey said. He looked real sick.

"Yes, today," he said.

"That's exactly right," Ruth said to Lynn. "She *is* my daughter, and I don't want her signing. I'm sure it's fun to learn a few words to use with your uncle and the chimp, but . . ."

"What?" Joey said, having missed some of her mother's response.

Ruth didn't repeat it, so Joey moved so she could see all their mouths.

"Fun," Charlie snapped. "Sign for fun." He heaved himself up and put his hand against the wall for support. "She's deaf, Mrs. Willis. She needs to learn to sign to survive."

Lynn tried to get him to sit down again, but Charlie jerked his arm away from her.

"People will stare. They'll pity her. Now at least she looks normal," her mother said, but her face showed no anger. Joey thought that was strange until she realized her mother must also be worried about the way Charlie looked.

"My parents were normal," he said. "And staring is just unfamiliarity with the language, like listening closely to someone speak French. It's not pity. It's curiosity."

Too late, her mother's hand flew to cover her mouth. She'd forgotten Charlie's parents had been deaf. "I'm sorry, I didn't mean normal in that sense of the word," she said. "I just want her to function in the hearing world. Hearing people don't sign."

"I'm hearing," Charlie said. "What's the real reason you don't want her to sign?"

Lynn clamped a hand over his. "This has gone far enough."

"Not yet, it hasn't," Charlie said.

Ruth stiffened. "I just told you the real reason."

"I don't think you have. People would watch her express herself with her beautiful hands and the whole world would know that your child is deaf. I don't know why that scares you so."

Ruth looked at Joey, eyes narrow. "You told him, didn't you?"

"I . . . I told him it *was* meningitis," Joey stammered.

"Is that what she told you?" her mother asked.

"It is. But I've seen the scars behind her ears. Meningitis doesn't leave scars. How did she really lose her hearing?"

Ruth hadn't believed her when Joey told her that she hadn't told him the truth. Now Charlie had confirmed it. A little of the fight left her mother's face at the same time as an odd expression crossed Charlie's. When he shook his head, Joey knew he'd figured it out. "You don't want her to use sign language because you are protecting yourself, not your daughter."

"That's a lie," her mother shouted.

"No," Charlie said. "It's the truth. You feel it's your fault that she's deaf."

"I didn't have anything to do with her deafness," her mother said. "It . . . it was meningitis."

"No, it wasn't, Mrs. Willis. Was it your ex-husband?"

Her mother's reaction filled in the part Joey missed. She grabbed blindly for the sofa to keep from falling.

"Charlie, please stop," Joey said. "It's okay. I manage."

Charlie took Joey's hand. "Managing isn't good enough."

Lynn patted Joey's back, then stepped around the coffee table and put her arm around Ruth's shoulders.

Her mother's head came up and she shook Lynn off. "Get out," she said to Charlie.

"No, I won't. This may be her only chance and I may be the only person who understands enough to tell you the truth. You're denying your daughter a full life. You have the chance to be brave now. Admit to yourself the reason you don't want her to sign is because more people will wonder how it happened. Don't you see that what you tell them isn't important, but what you tell Joey is. You are cutting her off from the rest of the world."

Ruth's head jerked as if she'd been slapped. "That's not true. I just want her life to be as normal as possible. I don't want people to feel sorry for her, to treat her differently."

"Deafness *is* different, dammit. And for Joey it is normal not to hear. But she's missing so much more because you're trying to pound her deaf ears into hearing holes. She is what she is. Let her be deaf."

Ruth sank to the sofa and looked pleadingly at Lynn. "He has no right."

"I know he doesn't."

Charlie lowered himself into Ray's chair, put his head back, and closed his eyes. "You two don't know what it's like for her. I do."

Ruth was still on the sofa, sobbing into her hands, when Ray's truck came down the drive. He came toward the house smiling, happy to see Charlie's car, no doubt. His expression sobered when he saw them all through the front window: Charlie in Ray's chair, pale as old decking, and Lynn and Joey on either side of Ruth, trying to comfort her.

Ruth hadn't seen him coming and started violently when the door opened. Ray's reaction to seeing her so anguished was to throw Charlie a questioning look, which didn't last. He must have asked if Charlie was okay, because Charlie said, "I'm fine," and introduced Lynn.

Ray's ruddy cheeks reddened and he wiped his calloused, knobby-fingered hand on his pants before putting it in hers.

"We're sorry," Lynn said. "I'm afraid Uncle Charlie has stuck his nose where it doesn't belong, but he's very fond of your daughter and . . ."

Whatever Ray said was lost to Joey, but her mother's head came up with a jerk. Lynn looked surprised and Charlie nodded.

"What did he say?" Joey asked, looking from one to the other.

"Have you ever understood anything Ray said?" Charlie asked.

Joey shook her head. "I can't see his mouth."

"Nothing? Ever?" Lynn asked. She looked stunned.

"No."

Ruth took Joey's hand. "Ray said, 'It's about time.' " She looked at Ray. "Have I really been that wrong?"

At first he shrugged, but then he nodded.

She turned back to Joey. "I didn't do it for any other reason than I thought it was what was best. I need you to believe that."

"I do, Mom."

Later that evening, when Joey slipped back into her room from her shower, she noticed that one of her pillows was higher, as though an animal had crawled up beneath it. Since her sliding glass door was always open a crack large enough that she'd once surprised a young raccoon in her room, she thought something might have crept in and hidden there. She approached it cautiously, jerked the pillow away, and jumped back. Beneath it was a crinkled brown paper sack with a note from Ray scrawled on the outside, *I found this at a yard sail a coupel weaks ago. Yur mother don't no. Don't tell her just yet.*

Inside the bag was a worn paperback copy of the *American Sign Language Concise Dictionary.* Joey hugged it to her chest and began to cry.

Chapter Eight

The months passed. The air got drier. Salamanders disappeared from beneath rotting logs and winter woodpiles, back into their summer burrows, trading places, it seemed, with the lizards and garter snakes that had spent the winter sleeping underground. Everything rushed to bloom: the flowers she and her mother planted in March, as well as the weeds, English daisies, wild geraniums, clover, and dandelions. Only when Ray or Joey mowed did their yard look, with all the flower heads lopped off, like the lawn her mother wished for.

School ended in early June. Joey passed the eighth grade, though just barely. Except for visiting Charlie, playing with Sukari, and missing Kenny, who promised to write from Maine, where he spent the summers, she imagined herself passing yet another summer dreading the coming of fall, and wishing she never had to go back to school again.

Smells were keys to Joey, unlocking memories. The smell of Mercurochrome always reminded her of waking in the Reno hospital, her head wrapped in bandages. The stink of stale beer or a dirty ashtray made her heart race. So, although it was now okay for her to continue teaching herself to sign, she did it in the privacy of her room or on her tree stump or at Charlie's, anywhere her mother wasn't likely to be openly confronted with the fact that she was still at it. She was afraid, just as the smell of warm, sunlit air reminded her of walking Charlie and Lynn to his car, that seeing her signing would remind her mother of that painful day.

One afternoon shortly after school let out for the summer, Ruth came home from work with a load of groceries. On top of one of the bags was the mail, which included a College of the Redwoods schedule of summer classes.

"Are you going to take another class?" Joey asked, as she helped unload the canned goods.

"Nope. You are."

"Huh?"

"They've got a summer-session sign language class. Do you want me to see if they'll let you take it?"

Joey bit her lip, then hugged her mother. "Oh, yes, please."

Ruth nodded with her lips compressed. "It's every day for six weeks."

"I don't care. And you don't have to take me; I can ride my bike down."

"No, I'll drive you."

Joey opened her mouth to say, *I'm nearly fourteen, Mom,* but caught herself. "You can if you want to, but I'll ride facing traffic and cross the highway at the light."

"All right. All right. I'll register you on my way to work Monday."

As it turned out, Joey was too young to enroll in a college class, so, to avoid the red tape of having to fill out forms and get the dean's approval, her mother enrolled in the class herself and Joey attended using her name.

On the first day, Joey misjudged how long it would take to ride the four and a half miles to school and arrived a few minutes late to find them sitting in a big semi-circle practicing signing their names. When Joey slipped in and took an empty desk, the teacher smiled and pointed to the board where she'd written, *No Talking* and *My name is Martha Alexander.* She then signed what she'd written.

Joey nodded.

When her turn came, Joey fingerspelled her own name without thinking. Ms. Alexander was checking each student off in her roll book. HAVE R-U-T-H W-I-L-L-I-S.

With heart pounding, Joey slowly answered, MY NAME J-O-E-Y R-U-T-H W-I-L-L-I-S.

OKAY. Ms. Alexander checked her name off, smiled, and pointed to the next student, who was fingerspelling her name when she glanced back at Joey. She brought an index finger to her ear then around to rest against her lips before pointing at Joey. DEAF YOU?

YES.

UNDERSTAND A-S-L YOU?

LITTLE BIT, Joey answered.

HAPPY YOU HERE, J-O-E-Y R-U-T-H.

Joey bit her lip.

After class, she waited at Ms. Alexander's desk until everyone else had left. She kept her head bowed and drew arcs on the carpet with the toe of her shoe until Ms. Alexander tapped her shoulder.

QUESTION?

Joey took a deep breath. "No, ma'am. I . . . I just want to tell you something."

Ms. Alexander waited.

"My name isn't Joey Ruth. I mean it is Joey, but Ruth is my mother's name. I just finished eighth grade."

TALL YOU.

Joey nodded. "I'm using her name."

When Ms. Alexander's eyes narrowed, Joey thought she was a goner, but instead she turned, uncapped the marker, and wrote, *You are welcome however you got here.*

On the second day, Ms. Alexander asked the other students to explain why they were taking the class. As they answered, she showed them the signs, then numbered and wrote each reason on the board:

1. *New friend deaf.*
2. *Uncle deaf.*
3. *Father is losing his hearing.*
4. *Thinks it's cool to talk with my hands.*

So it went around the room. Mostly they each had someone with whom they wished to talk. But when it was the turn of the young woman sitting directly across the room from Joey, she didn't answer. Instead she looked at Joey and tried to smile, then suddenly signed, SORRY, brought her hands to her eyes, and began to cry.

The woman in the desk next to her reached and squeezed the younger woman's shoulder. Ms. Alexander put her hand up for everyone to wait. After a minute the woman wiped her eyes on the tissue someone handed her. She must have given her reason for being there when the tissue obscured her mouth, because Ms. Alexander began to show her the signs she needed.

The young woman nodded, looked at Joey, and signed, MY BABY BORN DEAF.

Out of the corner of her eye, Joey saw Ms. Alexander add it to the growing list on the board: *9. Baby born deaf.*

All eyes turned to Joey as if they expected her to say something, but Ms. Alexander just pointed to the next person, who said she needed a second language to graduate. She blushed, then glanced first at the young woman with the deaf baby, then at Joey, before going on. "I thought ASL looked easier than French or Spanish because I already know how to speak English."

Ms. Alexander broke her own rule. "It's not easier," she said. "It will be just as difficult as any other language you study." *10. Need a second language.*

When it was Joey's turn, she realized she'd broken into a sweat. Her palms and her underarms were wet, but she swallowed and instead of answering, *I'm here because I'm deaf,* she looked across at the young woman. "I wasn't born deaf," she said, "so sometimes I imagine I still hear the sounds I remember, but I have a friend whose mother was born deaf and his father lost his hearing when he was two. His mother's family all learned to sign, and eventually his father learned it, too. I know Charlie would say you are doing the right thing for your baby."

Joey made no attempt to stop the tears that slid down her cheeks when Ms. Alexander wrote, *14. So I can talk to the people I love.*

After class, the young woman came and hugged Joey and thanked her. A few other students came and signed, MY NAME . . . and NICE MEET YOU.

After school each day, Joey went straight to Charlie's. The minute Sukari heard the squeal of her bike brakes, she'd appear at the front window hooting and signing, J-Y HERE. HURRY, HURRY. The second an exhausted-looking Charlie unlocked the door, she was out and into the milk basket Ray had wired to Joey's handlebars for what became their daily ride home to play with Luke.

One afternoon Joey was sitting, as usual, in the yard watching Sukari and Luke play cowboy and Indian when Ray came home from the mill with two newly hatched, nearly dead Canada geese. Ruth interpreted for Joey as he explained that he'd found them lying at the muddy edge of the mill's pond on Georgia-Pacific's four-hundred-acre oceanfront property.

Over her mother's objections, and with Sukari and Luke at her elbow, Joey lined her bathtub with newspapers and got an old yard-sale heating pad from the closet. She made them a bed on it under a cardboard box with a hole cut in the side so they could get in and out for food and water.

Ray called Charlie and he said, for the evening, just scramble them some eggs. Neither ate and in the morning, one was dead.

When Joey and Sukari came home the next day after school, the other one was running around and around in the tub, peeping and pooping.

Sukari was astonished. BIRD MAKE DIRTY, she signed, more or less to herself, every time the little goose pooped. She and Luke hung over the side and watched it for a long time until Luke got bored. But even his signing, TICKLE-CHASE, couldn't get Sukari to leave her post by the tub.

By the end of the week, the gosling was three times the size it had been when Ray found it. Joey'd never seen anything grow that fast. "It's like finding a different goose in there every afternoon," she told her mother.

As far as Sukari was concerned, the goose was hers, and vice versa. One day Joey decided it was time to teach *him*—the gender that Luke had assigned him since there was no way to tell if it was a girl or a boy—how to find his own food. With Luke and Sukari at her heels and Ray and Ruth watching from the doorway, she carried the kicking, foot-tall goose outside and put him down in a patch of dandelions. The second his little webbed feet touched the ground, he ran in orbits around first one tree, then another, his wing-nubs held out for balance. Sukari signed, CHASE ME, BIRD, and somehow timed one of his loops to get in front of him. From that moment on, where Sukari went, the goose named Gilbert followed.

A four-foot-high culvert ran from side to side beneath Morgan Creek Drive. The year-round cascade of water through it had formed a shallow pool on their side of the road. Each afternoon, Joey arrived home with Sukari and let the goose out of the cage Ray had built for him. While she changed into shorts and a T-shirt, Sukari and Luke helped Gilbert find bugs to eat. Sukari tipped up pots, beneath which sow bugs and ear- wigs hid. She'd eat a few sow bugs, but earwigs had pincers, so she left them for Gilbert. She also picked dandelion leaves for him; she ate the flowers.

The trail to the pool started on the far side of the yard. It curved to parallel the slope of the road bed, then doglegged right, down to the creek. The minute the goose heard the screen door slam and saw Joey come out of the house, he started across the yard, feet slapping the ground in a roly-poly run. Sukari followed, shedding her T-shirt and diaper on the way. Luke, who lived in his cowboy outfit, would peel off his vest, gun belt, shirt, cowboy hat, and chaps, to arrive last in his boots and bare-bottomed. It was all Joey could do to finish stripping him before they plunged into the icy water, screaming, while the goose swam in circles, then bathed, showering them with water.

When Gilbert started to fly, it was clear that his days living surrounded by a redwood forest were numbered, but Joey stalled releasing him until school started in August. Late in the afternoon, on the first Saturday after classes began, they all drove to the manmade pond on a small cattle farm in Caspar, a tiny town seven miles south of Fort Bragg. Dozens of Canada geese arrived there each evening to spend the night floating, safe from raccoons and foxes, in the middle of the pond.

Joey's biggest concern was how Sukari would react—whether she would let them leave her goose there. They rode to the pond in Ray's truck, Gilbert sitting in Joey's lap, a hotel shoe-polishing mitt over his head to keep him calm.

Other Canada geese were feeding at the pond, as were an assortment of domestic geese. People came every day to feed them, so when they pulled off the road, all the geese came running to the cattle fence.

Ray lifted Gilbert over the fence, but the sight of all the other geese frightened him. He ran, lifted off, and flew out into the middle of the pond. Sukari screamed, leapt out of Joey's arms, bolted over the fence, and charged the strange geese, which scattered in a panic.

Sukari loped along the levee that contained the pond until she was as close as she could get to where Gilbert floated. Joey had gone over the fence after her, but she stopped when Sukari did.

COME BIRD, Sukari signed.

Gilbert swam straight to her and walked out of the water. Sukari squatted down and slipped her arms under his wings. Joey glanced back at Ruth, Ray, and Luke, smiling.

"Look," her mother said, pointing.

Sukari was sitting on the levee, her arms still wrapped beneath Gilbert's wings, but he'd snuggled into her lap and lain his head and neck over Sukari's shoulder.

When Joey called, Gilbert followed Sukari back to the truck and they all drove home again. The next weekend, without Sukari, they took Gilbert to a man in Little River. He had five other tame Canada geese and a twenty-acre pond.

For a month afterward, the first thing Sukari would ask when Joey came over was, GO SEE BIRD? And if they went to play with Luke, Sukari ran straight to Gilbert's cage, signing, WHERE BIRD?

The first time she asked, Joey told her he'd flown away, but Sukari didn't understand what that meant. Eventually, Joey just said she didn't know, which was kind of the truth, and after a while Sukari gave up and quit asking. For a long time, Joey believed she'd forgotten, until they were sitting in the yard one day when Sukari suddenly looked up and began to scream. Joey glanced up in time to see a flock of geese disappear over the treetops. They were headed north, flying in formation. Sukari watched them go, signing, COME BIRD, until they were out of sight. She watched the sky for a few more minutes, then turned. BIRD GO, NEW FRIEND, she signed, then crawled into Joey's lap.

Near the end of September, Ruth asked, rather unenthusiastically, if Joey wanted a party for her fourteenth birthday, which was on October 19. To her mother's obvious relief, Joey said no. Whom would she invite, except Charlie, Sukari, and maybe Kenny, though he'd come back from Maine madly in love with some girl he'd met there?

At Charlie's that weekend, he, too, asked if she wanted a party.

Joey shook her head. "Not really. There's no one to invite."

"What are we, chopped liver?"

She grinned. "You know what I mean."

Charlie had let a few of his zucchinis grow to the size of small watermelons. He was cutting one into half-inch-thick slabs, which Joey was dipping a slice at a time into beaten eggs. Sukari was getting a lot of flour on herself and some on both sides of

each slice of zucchini. They were following an eggplant par-
mesan recipe, but since neither of them liked eggplant, they
were substituting zucchini. *Well, I like a good party,* Charlie
wrote, after he rinsed and put away the knife. *And since I
don't know how old the Dirty Diaper Devil is, I think the
19th would be a good day for her to turn four, so how
about I throw a party for her and you can stop by if you're
in the neighborhood.*

"You don't have to do this."

"I want to." *I'm an old man. How many of your birth-
days can I expect to see?*

"All of them, I hope."

As it turned out, that weekend happened to be a good one
for Lynn and her new husband to get away. A man, Charlie as-
sured Joey, couldn't possibly be good enough for her.

On the Wednesday before the party, Ruth picked Joey up at
the speech therapist and took her to Spunky Skunk, the toy
store in town, where she spent most of her allowance for a
large box of crayons and a big coloring book full of bird pictures, including one of a Canada goose.

Though Ruth, in her way, had clearly gotten attached to
Sukari over the summer, she drew the line at spending "hard-
earned money" on a present for a chimpanzee. Joey was just
happy she had agreed to go, since she still bore a grudge against
Charlie. Though Ray had gone over a number of times to watch
baseball or golf, her mother had rejected every invitation he'd
extended, nor had she let Joey take Luke.

After showing Luke Sukari's room and her tortoise, Joey left
them to put one of Luke's old ten-piece puzzles of a German

shepherd together. It was the "gift" her mother brought wrapped in an old Harvest Market grocery bag, which advertised the annual Fourth of July salmon barbecue.

Though Charlie had been set to dislike Lynn's husband, it turned out to be impossible. He, like Lynn, was a doctor, a cardiologist, with a big wide grin like Sukari's. His name was Jack, which he knelt and fingerspelled slowly for Sukari after he noticed her trudging along at his heels signing, NAME YOU MAN? over and over.

"I only married him for your benefit," Lynn told Charlie. "We needed somebody in the family who can keep you and your old ticker in line."

"Hmph," was Charlie's reply.

After she and Sukari blew out the candles—fourteen on Joey's half and four on Sukari's—and finished having carrot cake and ice cream, Joey went to sit on the deck with the adults mostly as company for her mother, who she knew felt uncomfortable. She had come to the party only because it was Joey's birthday, but she sat separately from the others, gazing off into the woods and speaking only when spoken to. Joey was trying to track the conversation when her mother suddenly jumped up and ran into the house. Everyone rushed after her.

Luke was crying and Sukari was standing on the couch throwing magazines and crayons at the puzzle.

"What's the matter with you," Charlie snapped at Sukari.

"Did she bite you?" Ruth asked Luke, which, by her face, she instantly regretted asking. They'd played together all summer and not bitten each other.

Sukari scrambled into Charlie's arms, where she continued to scream and point at the puzzle.

"Oh, that's it." Charlie covered the puzzle with a cushion. "She's afraid of dogs." He patted her back. "Since I've had her, she's never seen a dog, so I think that must be how they treed and killed her mother."

Sukari stuck her lips out and signed, BAD, BITE SUKARI. Her forehead crinkled and her eyes widened.

After asking Joey if she minded, Lynn tore two pages from the coloring book and made Sukari and Luke sit together and draw. Luke scribbled for a few minutes, then ran to Ruth with his picture. Joey saw Sukari look up and watch as Ruth held it for everyone to admire, then hugged and kissed him. Sukari scribbled another minute, then came out onto the deck, dragging her picture.

Joey expected she'd take it to Charlie or herself, but she carried it straight to Ruth.

Throughout the summer, Sukari had kept her distance from Ruth, so her mother tensed a bit when Sukari laid it on her lap and poked her picture with a finger. GOOD GIRL ME, she signed. HUG.

When Joey interpreted, Ruth smiled. She leaned over. "This is the best one," she said close to Sukari's ear, and, just as she had done for Luke, she held it for everyone to see, then patted Sukari's head.

Sukari waited a moment, then signed, HUG.

"She wants a hug, Mom," Joey said. "Like Luke got."

"Oh . . . well . . . I don't know." Ruth glanced around.

Everyone was watching and smiling. "She's a little person, isn't she?"

HUG, Sukari signed again, then held her arms up.

Ruth reached over, put her hands under Sukari's arms, and lifted her into her lap. She hugged the little chimp and kissed the top of her head.

Joey glanced at Ray, who winked at her and smiled.

Chapter Nine

On an uncommonly warm night in April, Joey awoke from a dream of being adrift at sea in a small boat to find herself gripping the sides of her bed, which heaved and bucked beneath her. She sat bolt upright. *Earthquake.* She grinned. The framed poster that Charlie had given her for her birthday of Koko, the sign-language-using gorilla, and her kitten, All Ball, swung on its nail. Her little vibrating alarm clock, which was on the nightstand, duck-walked to the edge and fell off. *This is so cool,* she thought for a second before her ceiling fan came loose. Joey pulled her legs up and covered her head, but the fan fell only the length of its cord, then swung in wide, slow circles just inches above the bed. The redwood limbs, just visible in the gray light of morning, swayed here and there, up and down. Then, as suddenly as it had started, her bed stopped moving.

Joey jumped up. The chest in the hall had fallen against her door and she hit her shin on it. She lifted it back up against the wall and cut through the bathroom to Luke's room where she spotted his two little legs sticking out from beneath his bed.

Her heart leapt. "Are you okay?" She grabbed his ankles and pulled him out.

He was crying and she hugged him. "It's okay, honey. We had an earthquake. It's over now," she said.

"Mommy," he wailed when he saw the flashlight beam swaying down the dark staircase from Ruth and Ray's room.

Ray had a lump above his left eye, which was already darkening.

Ruth squeezed around him. "Are you two all right?"

"We're fine," Joey said.

They were all smiling and laughing with relief when the house began to shake again.

"Aftershock," Ruth said calmly, but she grabbed Ray's arm.

The kitchen was a wreck. The bottom cupboards had had child-proof latches on them from the time Luke started to crawl, but the upper cabinets had flown open and nearly all the dishes, glasses, spices, herbs, and canned goods were on the floor. There was broken glass everywhere, splattered with Newman's Own spaghetti sauce, which made the mess look bloody.

Joey knelt to hold a garbage bag open while Ray shoveled the broken glass into it. When he suddenly dropped the dustpan and went to the front door, the hair on the back of Joey's neck prickled. She scrambled to her feet and ran after him.

Only the top half of their door was glass, so it looked as if no one was there, but Ray unlocked and jerked it open as if the house were on fire. It was Sukari.

She screamed, flailed her arms, and spun in circles. The instant Ray opened the screen door, she charged into the room and into Joey's arms.

"What are you doing here?" Joey said, looking out at the driveway. "Where's Turtle?" She looked at her mother, then at Ray. "No," she cried when she saw the expressions on their faces.

With Sukari slung on her hip, Joey ran down the trail. A hundred yards from the house, a tree had fallen, blocking her way.

Sukari weighed twenty-three pounds last time Joey had put her on the scale, but she felt heavier. Joey stopped for a second to gasp for air, shifted Sukari to the other hip, and climbed up through the trees. When she got to Charlie's, Ray and her mother and Luke were pulling into the driveway. Ray ran and pounded on the front door. There was no answer and the door was locked.

Joey ran down the side of the house and up the back steps. Sukari's jungle gym had fallen through a pane of the sliding glass door. Joey stepped inside and crossed through the broken glass. When she put Sukari down, the little chimp darted down the hall and disappeared into a rear bedroom.

Charlie was on the floor beside his bed, his right hand clutching the front of his pajama top. Joey screamed for her mother and Ray, then turned to find them in the doorway. Ray knelt and pressed his fingers to the side of Charlie's throat, turned, and said something to Ruth.

"Is he dead?" Joey cried.

Ray shook his head, no.

Sukari had crawled between Charlie and the bed and was touching his eyelids softly with one finger and signing to him with the other hand.

Ruth grabbed the phone and punched 911. "The ambulance

is coming," she said and hung up. "What's she doing?" she asked Joey, trying to shoo Sukari away from Charlie. "Why is she grinning like that?"

Joey was hunkered at Charlie's feet, rocking on her heels. She looked at Sukari and realized she was signing, J-Y HERE, J-Y HERE, and trying to pick his eyes open.

"She's scared and trying to tell him I'm here." Tears rolled down Joey's cheeks. "I am here, Charlie."

After a moment, Charlie's eyes blinked open. He smiled weakly. "So you are," he said, then cupped Sukari's face in his palm. "You're a good girl."

"An ambulance is on the way, Charlie," Ruth said. "You hang on."

"Too late," he said and closed his eyes.

Sukari signed, TURTLE SLEEP, then lay beside him and closed her eyes for a second before lifting her head to peek at him.

Joey squeezed his foot. "Charlie, don't say that. Sukari needs you. I need you."

Only his fingers moved. He lifted the index finger of the fist at his chest and pointed to Sukari, then pointed his open hand to Joey. "Take care of her."

"I will 'til you're better. I promise."

His lips moved. "I love my girls."

Joey looked from her mother to Ray. "Why are you sitting there?" she cried. "Can't you help him?"

Ruth knelt and put an arm around Joey. "There's nothing we can do, honey."

"There must be something. CPR, or something."

Joey grabbed his hand. "Charlie, please wait."

Charlie folded his fingers around her hand. A single tear appeared in the corner of his right eye and slid free with his last breath.

"Charlie," Joey cried, tugging his hand. "Oh, Charlie. Please."

Ruth tried to pull her away. "It's over, honey," she said.

"No." She looked pleadingly from one to the other. "Ray?"

When tears filled her stepfather's eyes, Joey slumped against the side of the bed and pulled Sukari into her arms. "What will I do without him?" she sobbed against the coarse hair of her thin shoulder.

Ruth walked Luke home while Ray waited on the front steps with his head in his hands for the ambulance to take Charlie's body to the hospital. Joey sat with Sukari in her lap and held Charlie's hand. Every couple of minutes, Sukari would tug gently on Charlie's pajama sleeve until finally she leaned over with Joey's arms around her waist for support and stared intently at his face. She brushed his eyelashes with a finger, then turned and signed, TURTLE SLEEP. Joey could only nod.

When Ray came to the bedroom door, Joey knew the ambulance had arrived.

WANT BATH? she asked Sukari, who hooted with joy and ran down the hall, stripping off her pajama top and diaper as she went.

Joey had no idea how long she'd been sitting with Sukari and Hidey, both napping among the litter of toys, books, and dolls that Sukari had dragged up to surround them on the sofa, but when her mother's hand on her shoulder startled her, the sun had moved to cast long shadows on the deck.

"I thought I'd call Lynn," she said. "Do you know her number?"

Joey shook her head. "Did you look on his desk?"

"It's a mess in there."

"Her last name is Mansell, too, and she lives in Fresno." She started to get up, but Sukari screamed when she moved.

"Stay there," Ruth said.

Joey hugged Sukari. "I won't leave you."

Charlie's moth-eaten old sweater was slung across the back of the couch. Joey picked it up and buried her nose in it. It smelled so strongly of him that it was hard to believe he wasn't there. Tears came again. She wiped her arm across her eyes and put the sweater around Sukari's shoulders.

Her mother came and sat in Charlie's recliner and twirled a strand of her hair around her index finger. She often did that while watching television, sometimes inspecting the tips and pinching off the split ends. Joey wondered how everything could continue to look and smell the same.

Her mother waved for her attention. "Lynn will be here Friday."

"Why so long?"

"One of her patients is due."

"Who?"

"Not who, due. A baby is coming."

Joey nodded.

"She was awfully upset."

"Charlie was like a father to her."

Her mother slid forward in the chair. "I've called Animal Control."

Joey stiffened and watched her mother's mouth more closely. "What's that?"

"People to take Sukari until Lynn . . ."

"No."

"She can't stay here."

"Why not? I'll stay with her."

"Alone? No way."

"Why?"

"You're deaf, Joey. If you're not standing right under it, you can't even hear a smoke alarm." She pointed to the unit attached to the ceiling.

Joey opened her mouth to protest, but her mother held up her hand. "You can't hear the phone."

"So? I can call out." She thought of what Charlie had written in her sign language book. Tears pooled in her eyes. "I'm deaf, not helpless, Mom."

Her mother looked past her toward the front door, then got up. "I said no. That's final."

A young woman in a beige uniform left a large carry-cage just outside the door before stepping into the foyer. She smiled at Joey. "I've never picked up a monkey before."

"She's deaf," her mother said.

"Oops, sorry," said the woman.

Joey had seen her say "monkey." "She's not a monkey."

The woman glanced back and forth between Joey and her mother.

"She reads lips."

"Oh, of course. Will she bite?" the woman asked Joey, making each word big.

Sukari moved in tight to Joey's legs, hair bristling as if she, too, had taken an instant dislike to this woman. SUKARI BITE, she signed.

Joey almost smiled. "Yes, she'll bite."

"Has she ever bitten anyone?" The woman spoke quickly. "We have a policy. If she's bitten anyone, we'll have to destroy her."

"What's she saying?" Joey demanded.

"Nothing," her mother said; then said to the woman, "She minds my daughter."

"Good, good," the woman said, moving farther into the room. "Oh, look, she's smiling."

All of Sukari's teeth showed.

"That's not a smile," Joey said. "She's scared."

Sukari moved to put Joey between herself and the woman, who came around the end of the sofa and slipped a syringe from her pocket. "Can you hold her?" she asked Joey.

Joey usually liked people with easy lips to read, but not this woman. "Leave her alone," she said, then glanced pleadingly at her mother.

"This will put her to sleep."

"No."

The woman turned to Ruth.

"Joey, help her catch Sukari. It's for her own good."

"Liar," Joey screamed.

Ruth's hand flew and the open palm caught Joey's cheek. The smell of tobacco was so strong on her mother's stained fingers that the odor lingered in the air between them. Joey was stunned. Her mother had never hit her. She touched her cheek where it stung.

"Oh Jesus, I'm sorry," Ruth said. The back of her hand flew to her mouth.

Joey straightened her usually humped shoulders to make herself taller before turning to the woman. "You're not taking her. Charlie said she was mine. Those were his last words. You can't have her if I say you can't."

Her mother's hand waved desperately. "Don't be ridiculous," she said. "He didn't mean for *you* to keep her."

Sukari took Joey's hand. She could smell Charlie's sweater, which Sukari had pulled over her head.

"Yes, he did."

"Where do you plan to keep her?" her mother asked, her face full of sarcasm.

There had been no time to think of that. Joey shrugged. "I don't know, but you can't put her in a cage. She has her own room like Luke and I do. Don't you understand, Mom? I'm not going to let anyone"—Joey glanced at the woman who was filling the syringe from a bottle in her pocket—"take her from the only home she knows. I'll stay here with her until Lynn comes."

"It may be weeks before Lynn can take her. Or maybe she won't want her."

"Lynn will take her. She loves Sukari. So does Jack."

Ruth looked at them, then at the woman, whom, Joey realized, her mother didn't like, either. When she said, "We'll try it for one night," Joey knew she had won.

The woman looked disappointed. "Want me to take the cat?"

They all turned to follow her gaze. Hidey had gone up the drapes and was crouched on the valance.

Sukari gave a hoot and would have scampered up after him if Joey hadn't caught her around the waist. "Not the cat, either," she said to her mother.

After Joey swept up the broken glass, she tried to entertain Sukari, who would sit quietly for a few minutes before running down the hall to Charlie's room, then to the bathroom, then to his office. WHERE TURTLE? she'd demanded after each search.

Joey had no idea how to tell her the truth. Did Sukari remember her mother being killed or Charlie's wife dying? Could she understand what death meant? "He's here," she said finally, tapping Sukari's chest, then her own. "This is where he lives now," she added, sinking into the soft cushions of the sofa. She put her head back and closed her eyes and soon felt Sukari crawl up beside her. When she peeked, the little chimp was sitting with her head back and her eyes closed, too.

After only a moment or two, Sukari scrambled down but this time she ran to the front door.

It was Ray. He waved, then maneuvered a large sheet of plywood through the opening. He had cut it to fit the shattered sliding glass door.

Though Joey had never spent an entire day in charge of Sukari, she was familiar with her tricks. Like any child, Sukari went from one game to another, losing interest almost as quickly as she started something new. Joey was exhausted and wished she'd settle on something quiet and stick with it, but each time

Joey tried to get her to finish a puzzle or draw a picture, Sukari would rub her thumb and index finger together: her sign for "raisin."

For a while Joey gave them to her. She wanted Sukari to be quiet so that she could think about Charlie, collect her memories. "You've had enough raisins," Joey said, when she realized Sukari had eaten an entire eight-ounce box.

By evening, Sukari had such horrible diarrhea that Joey took her diaper off and carried one of her potties with them from room to room.

Her mother showed up at dinnertime with Joey's pajamas, her toothbrush, and a Papa Murphy's Hawaiian pizza, Joey's favorite because she loved pineapple. So did Sukari, who plucked and ate most of them before the oven heated up.

When Joey mentioned bedtime, Sukari ran to her room. *That was easy,* Joey was thinking, when Sukari came back in to the living room trailing her wagon, into which she'd piled a selection of games and toys.

"I don't think so," Joey said, took the wagon, and wheeled it back into Sukari's room. When she came back, Sukari had disappeared.

Joey checked Charlie's room, then the bathroom. As she crossed the living room to look in the office, she saw the draperies move and Sukari's long toes sticking out from beneath them. Joey tiptoed over to the chain that opened the curtains and drew them back to expose Sukari, pressed against the window with a jar of Skippy peanut butter. She grinned at Joey and offered up a gloppy finger full.

Joey scooped her up, carried her to the bathroom, and, to

Sukari's delight, ran another bath. Joey soaped her head, back, and belly, which she'd caked with peanut butter, while Sukari signed to her rubber animals and kicked her legs, soaking Joey to the skin. After the splashy, soapy ordeal, Sukari, wrapped in a towel, pulled her stool out and climbed up onto the edge of the bathroom counter. She got her toothbrush from the holder and squeezed out a big glob of Crest.

Joey cleaned the hair out of the tub. When she turned to throw it in the toilet, she saw Sukari, head back and mouth open, wringing out a long, delicious strand of toothpaste.

"Stop that." Joey grabbed the toothpaste away from her. "You make Luke look like an angel."

A little later Sukari crawled into Joey's lap with her hair-brush and sat like a princess, admiring herself in her hand-held mirror while Joey brushed her from head to toe. She kissed her reflection, then held it for Joey to admire, as if her image stayed on the glass.

When she'd been quiet for a while and seemed to be sleepy, Joey carried her to her room and helped her up onto her bed-board. Joey stood on the ladder and tucked the blanket around Sukari and covered her with Charlie's sweater. "I love you, sugar-butt," she whispered and kissed her cheek.

When she reached the door, she turned and blew her a kiss.

DOLL, Sukari signed.

Joey found a doll in the toy box and handed it up to her. When she reached the door again, Sukari signed, HAT, and pointed to her cowboy hat dangling from a hook on the back of the door.

Joey handed it up.

HUG.

Joey climbed up and hugged her.

This time she didn't look back when she reached the door, but when she flipped off the light, Sukari screamed loudly enough for Joey to hear.

She turned the light on. "What?"

BEAR.

"Okay. Okay." She tossed her her bear.

TRICYCLE.

"No way, you brat."

RAISIN.

"No."

HAIRBRUSH.

"This is the last thing." UNDERSTAND?

Joey was stretched out on the sofa, petting Hidey, who was asleep on her stomach, when Sukari's face appeared over the back of the couch. Joey jumped, scaring Hidey, who leapt away, scratching Joey's stomach clear through her sweatshirt.

"Now what?"

Sukari came around the end of the couch, dragging one of her potties. She grinned, in the dimness of the light above the stove. She pulled her diapers down, fastened her bottom to the potty, and pooped.

Joey went for tissue to wipe her, powdered her bottom, pulled her diaper up, then lay back down and patted her chest.

The day that had started with an earthquake ended with Sukari curled against Joey's side, the top of her head lodged beneath Joey's chin, asleep in each other's arms.

* * *

Lynn arrived on Friday. Joey followed Sukari to the door and let her in. They hugged until Lynn had to give in to Sukari's demand to be picked up. She signed, WHERE TURTLE? in Lynn's face.

WHAT TELL HER? Lynn asked.

"That he is here now." She tapped her chest. "I didn't know how to tell her the truth."

Lynn put Sukari down and took a pad from her purse. *It's best she doesn't know. Let's let her think she is going to my house to see him.*

Joey nodded. That was the first she knew for sure that Lynn was going to give Sukari a home. She was relieved and shattered. Lynn was going to take her, but take her away.

Lynn patted Joey's shoulder, then wrote, *You can see her anytime. Fresno's not very far from Fremont.* She smiled when Joey looked up.

"Fremont?"

I guess he didn't get a chance to tell you, did he?

"Tell me what? Where's Fremont?"

South of Oakland. Lynn took Joey's arm and led her to the sofa.

Sukari raced ahead and fished the dog puzzle from beneath a cushion. She drew her lips back and showed it to Lynn.

"Scary," Lynn said, then sat Joey down and wrote, *I don't want your mother to know that I told you, but Charlie just finished setting up a trust fund so you can go to the California School for the Deaf in Fremont. The school is free, as is room and board, but he's made it so your parents won't*

*have to pay a nickel for anything. The trust fund will buy
your clothes, pay your medical insurance, anything that the
state doesn't cover. There's even a generous allowance.*

Lynn reached over Joey's shoulder as she read and added,
It's a wonderful school!

Joey looked up from reading; tears brimmed, then spilled
down her cheeks. "Why would he do that?"

"He loved you, honey," Lynn said, then wrote, *He wanted
only the best for you.*

"Does Mom know?"

"Yes, and she said no." *But I think that was a knee-jerk
reaction,* Lynn wrote. *I think she'll change her mind.
Don't tell her you know. Anger will make it harder for her
to think it through, to realize what this means for you.
Right now, I think she feels Charlie has stolen you from
her, and that this extends his reach beyond the grave. She
needs to get past that.*

Lynn may have thought her mother would change her mind,
but Joey didn't. As she knelt in front of Sukari to tell her that
she was going with Lynn, Joey believed that they would drive
away and she would never see either of them again.

Joey took a small suitcase from the hall closet and went into
Sukari's room. Time seemed to slow to a crawl as she opened
it on the floor and began to fold Sukari's clothes, putting them
in piece by piece.

Sukari stood in the doorway and watched for a minute or so
before she ran in, pulled the clothes out, and threw them around
the room. Joey sat down in the middle of the floor. "Come sit
with me," she said.

One of the signs for "doctor" is to tap the pulse in the wrist with the "D" hand. Lynn's sign-name was the thumb of the "L" hand tapped against the pulse. Joey hugged Sukari, then made her watch as she signed, YOU GO L HER HOUSE.

Sukari broke free and ran circles around her, slapping her on the back each time she passed. Joey caught her arm and pulled her into her lap. SUKARI GO L HER HOUSE, Joey signed, then with a tightness in her chest that made it hard to breathe, she added, SEE TURTLE.

Sukari watched Joey's hands, then studied her face. SEE TURTLE?

Joey nodded.

J-Y GO?

Joey pulled Sukari close so that she couldn't see her tears. "Not just yet," she whispered.

In the end, they had to "slip her a mickey," as Lynn called it, with some tranquilizers she'd gotten from the Humane Society. Joey fed them to Sukari in a banana, then read to her until she was asleep. Joey lined the big carry-cage Lynn had brought with Sukari's blanket and folded Charlie's sweater for a pillow. She added her favorite animal book and her teddy bear, then carried Sukari to the car, but couldn't bring herself to put her down. She just stood there with her head bowed and her skin stinging in the cool air as if she'd been peeled. When Lynn touched her shoulder, Joey buried her face against her little friend's neck. "My heart is breaking," she whispered, then leaned and laid Sukari on the floor of the cage.

The last thing Lynn did before driving away was to nail a for-sale sign on a tree by the road. She stood with her arm around

Joey's shoulders and stared back at the house, wiping her eyes from time to time with the heel of her hand. Lynn had let Joey pick anything she wanted of Charlie's to keep. She took Sukari's tortoise and its aquarium for Luke and for herself chose his binoculars, the field guide he'd loaned her on their first walk in the woods, and a baby picture of Sukari taken in Africa. In it Charlie stood behind his wife, who held Sukari up to face the camera. But when the picture was snapped Sukari had twisted to reach for the baby bottle in Charlie's hand. The photo caught Charlie holding the bottle out of her reach like a torch as he leaned to kiss Sukari's forehead. At the same moment his wife, on her tiptoes, kissed his cheek.

On the second Monday after Lynn left with Sukari, Ruth, Joey, and Luke came home from school to find a strange man sitting in a BMW in front of their house. He stepped out as they came down the hill from the mailbox. He was dressed in a suit and tie, so Joey thought that he was a Jehovah's Witness, but it wasn't Saturday.

"He must be from out of town." She glanced at her mother. The angry expression on her mother's face surprised her and suggested that she knew who he was and why he was there. It only took a second more for her to figure out that this was Charlie's lawyer.

Joey nodded at the stranger and started for the house when out of the corner of her eye she saw him wave for her attention. Her mother looked grim.

The man handed both Joey and her mother a business card that read, BRYAN MCCULLY, ATTORNEY AT LAW, THE LAW OFFICES

OF MCCULLY, WHITNEY, AND SAMUELS, SAN FRANCISCO, CALI-
FORNIA. Joey started to hand the card back, but Mr. McCully
signed, KEEP, and then, USE A-S-L YOU?

YES, Joey signed, nervous that he might be as good as Charlie and would lose her if he signed too fast. LITTLE BIT, she
added.

Her mother folded her arms across her chest.

Mr. McCully opened his briefcase on the hood of his car and
took out a notepad. *I am Dr. Mansell's attorney,* he wrote.

Joey didn't say anything.

Mr. McCully glanced at her mother, then wrote, *Dr.
Mansell left his estate to his niece but he set up a special
trust for you: an education fund. You can go to the California School for the Deaf in Fremont free of charge, if
your parents are willing, and the trust will pay for all
your other expenses.*

He was smiling when Joey looked up from the note. "Really?" Joey said, and hoped she seemed surprised. She glanced
at her mother, who'd read the note over her shoulder. Her expression confused her. She didn't look mad anymore. Her face
showed no emotion at all; it was as blank as if she'd been told
a joke she didn't get. Joey risked the question: "Can I go?"

Ruth's face clouded. "I'm not going to decide that right this
minute. We'll talk about it later."

Mr. McCully had added more to his note: *There is also a
provision in the trust that will pay for your college education. There is Gallaudet in Washington, D.C., or California State University at Northridge.*

"Wow," Joey said. Lynn hadn't told her about college.

In addition, Dr. Mansell—

Joey's mother moved in suddenly and took her arm. "Go in the house. I want to talk to Mr. McCully alone."

Joey did as she was told but watched from the window, hoping to catch something of the conversation. Instead, her mother purposely maneuvered them so that they talked side by side facing away from her and toward the road. Joey crossed her fingers behind her back, but her heart sank when Mr. McCully shook his head, got into his car, and left without glancing back.

By the time her mother came into the house, Joey had gotten plates down and was setting the table. "Did he mention Sukari?" Joey asked.

"No."

"What did he say?"

Ruth opened the refrigerator door and stood staring at the contents for a full minute before closing it without taking anything out. She turned to face Joey. "You know what, I'm not ready to talk about this and I want you to accept that for now."

It was the first week of May. There was no sense pushing her mother. If she decided to let her go, it wouldn't be until September, anyway. Joey nodded and went back to setting three places for dinner.

Chapter Ten

Every year, on the weekend in June closest to the summer solstice, the neighbors gathered at one house for a potluck. This year it was the Willises' turn to host the party, which meant they provided the meat. Ray planned to smoke a turkey.

In preparation, Joey mowed the dry, brown weeds in their yard while Ray cleared a spot for the small bonfire at the edge of the gravel drive at a point farthest from any trees. He made a circle of plastic lawn chairs and two-foot-tall redwood rounds, then placed firewood nearby, though not the dry, clean, woodstove wood that he'd split himself. Instead, he collected and stacked cruddy wood, full of sow bugs, earwigs, and slugs. Luke helped by gathering twigs and small branches to use as kindling.

That afternoon, following the first greeting, no one made much effort to talk to Joey. She stood apart from the clutches of people chatting and watched Luke chase and be chased by the other neighborhood children. Once or twice, Joey saw him brush the back of his hand with his index finger, Sukari's sign for CHASE ME. It meant nothing to the other children, but Joey had to blink back tears. She wanted to close her eyes, open them again, and see Sukari race past with Luke on her heels; see Charlie sitting in the late afternoon sun, throw back his head and laugh.

As soon as the sun dipped behind the trees, the air grew chilly. Someone lit the fire and people began to slide closer to its warmth, backing up to it with their hands held behind them, palms to the flames.

The tradition was that everyone who played an instrument brought it for the after-dinner sing-along. While the children roasted chocolate-and-marshmallow-stuffed banana boats, the musicians sat on the redwood rounds and everyone else settled into the lawn chairs.

It was dark by the time the band of a harmonica, a fiddle, two guitars, an accordion, and a flute struck up. The Nadeaus had brought cheese and crackers on a tray made from an old washboard. Ron Nadeau had since rinsed it clean with the garden hose. He kept a rhythm strumming it while Gregory Smith slapped out the beat on the cardboard box his parents had carried the salad bowl in. In the middle of one of the livelier tunes, Luke dragged Lyle Nadeau out to dance.

Joey laughed and drummed randomly on her thighs until she saw her mother shake her head. "You're throwing off the beat."

"Sorry." Joey hunched her shoulders and jammed her hands between her knees.

Luke and Lyle went from dancing to chasing each other around the fire. When Ruth clapped her hands for them to stop, they began to dance again, doing something that resembled the twist, fists punching the space between them with each shift of their squat little bodies. The first time their fists bumped, they rolled into each other and fell to the ground, wrestling like bear cubs.

Ruth got up, pulled them apart, brushed the dust and ash from their bottoms, and shoved them out through the circle of singers and musicians to let them work it out in the yard. "Help me keep an eye on them," she said to Joey when she sat back down.

The music turned melancholy. Ruth and Gregory's sister, Katherine, began a song. The light from the fire flickered on the ring of faces, many with their eyes closed to listen—the opposite of how Joey heard.

Ruth and she were sharing space on a log. Joey shifted a bit so she could keep an eye on the boys playing in a bright patch of moonlight and still watch her mother. She had no memory of her mother's singing voice, so the words "if ever I would leave you, it wouldn't be in springtime" sounded spoken in her mind.

When she glanced at her mother again, Ruth's cheeks glistened in the firelight.

"Are you crying?"

Her mother shook her head. "Not really."

"Your face is wet. Is it a sad song?"

Ruth wiped beneath her eyes with the heels of her hands. "It's just an old song . . . popular when I was about your age."

"Did it make you sad back then?"

"No. It just reminded me of all the things I wanted to do with my life. I guess I never dreamed that I'd end up here . . ." she glanced around, "like this."

"This is a good place, isn't it?"

Ruth put a finger to her lips as she often did when Joey's voice rose too high in conversation. "This is a wonderful place. That's not it."

The next song started and her mother waved an end to the discussion. It was a lively tune and Gregory pounded the cardboard box; fingers flashed on the guitars and a bow whipped the fiddle strings. Joey put her palms flat against the log, trying to feel the subtle bass thump like she sometimes felt in her feet and chest from the stereo of a passing car. Her foot began to tap in the dust, but she stopped when she felt her mother watching her. Joey turned again to watch the boys.

Ruth tapped her shoulder. When Joey looked, her mother began to clap the rhythm. She smiled and her head bobbed in time. "Come on," she said.

Joey picked up the beat first with a foot, then with her hands until they smacked in time with her mother's.

The next morning, Ruth came out to where Joey raked the coals aside while Ray carried shovels full of ashes to spread around the flowerbeds.

"Fun last night, huh?" her mother said.

Joey nodded and smiled. "Is Luke still asleep?"

"Dead to the world," her mother said, then bit her lip. "Do you really want to go to the deaf school?"

With the question hanging between them, Joey, for the moment, wasn't sure it was what she wanted. She also knew that if she wavered, there might not be another chance. "Yes, Mom, I do."

"Then I think you should go."

Joey felt as if her heart had stopped midbeat. "You do?"

"I'll call Mr. McCully on Monday." She turned and started for the house, then stopped and came back.

She's gonna change her mind, Joey thought. *Or tell me she's still against it.*

But her mother took the rake from her and laid it on the ground, then she hugged her, tightly, before she let go and stepped back, holding both of Joey's hands in hers. "Charlie was right."

Ray, who had scooped another shovel full of ashes, stopped to listen.

Ruth began to tremble with emotion. "He was right . . ." Her grip had shifted to Joey's wrist and she groped for Ray's arm for added support with the other. "And he's given me a chance to change that." Tears streaked her face. She waved her hands, unable to continue. "I'm so sorry."

"Oh, Mom, don't cry." Joey hugged her. "It doesn't matter. Earlier would have been too soon."

Ray dropped the shovel and put his arms around them both, smiling broadly at Joey over the top of her mother's head.

Even though the California School for the Deaf was in Fremont, it wasn't going to be the huge move that they had thought it would be. Joey would live at the school during the week, but all students went home on weekends. It meant Ruth or Ray would have to drive the twisty road to Willits where the bus stopped twice each weekend, which they both swore they didn't mind doing.

On August 29th, with the backseat piled high with Joey's

clothes, she and her mother left for Fremont. They made it in five hours with a single stop for Kentucky Fried Chicken, which Joey hadn't tasted since they moved from Reno.

They stayed in a motel that first night and were met early the next morning, as scheduled, by two women: Bridgetta, a tiny woman with the prettiest face Joey had ever seen, and Tanya, a lovely, willowy woman who wore high heels and stood ramrod straight at well over six feet.

Ruth beamed at the very pregnant Bridgetta. "When is your baby due?"

Bridgetta smiled and signed, TWO-WEEKS, which Tanya repeated for Ruth.

"I'm sorry," Ruth said to Tanya. "I didn't know *she* was deaf."

Joey knew what it was like not to be addressed directly. She put a hand on her mother's arm. "Mom, Tanya is Bridgetta's interpreter."

"Yes, yes. I know that now."

"Bridgetta understood and answered you."

Ruth looked confused.

"Talk to her like you talk to me, Mom."

"Of course," she said to Tanya, then realized she was doing it again and turned to Bridgetta. "I'm sorry."

Bridgetta squeezed Ruth's hand, then signed, WANT BOY. She cupped the sides of her stomach, looked up, and smiled. HAVE MORE CHILDREN?

"A son," Ruth said, after Tanya interpreted. "Luke. He's four."

Even as early as it was, the temperature had already soared into the eighties as Joey and Ruth followed Bridgetta and Tanya on a tour of the tree-shaded campus, including the cafeteria, the theater, a few of the classrooms, and finally her dorm room in Building 9. Her roommate had not arrived, so Joey left her bags behind the door. She wanted to start off on the right foot by letting her choose whichever bed she wanted.

Joey loved the look of the school, loved the single-story dorm units, each about the size of their house before the upstairs addition. Though the large central living room was empty, she tried to imagine girls watching TV and studying at the desks. She tried to picture herself fixing pizza in the small kitchen, but the more she tried to see herself in this setting, the more overwhelmed she became.

Both Bridgetta and Tanya signed too quickly for her to understand more than a word here and there, and Tanya barely moved her lips when she spoke. Everything Bridgetta signed, Tanya interpreted for Ruth, then her mother had to repeat it for Joey. Here she was, where Charlie said she should be, at a school for deaf people, and she was beginning to think she'd be more isolated and alone than ever.

After their tour, she went to have her signing skills, which she considered pathetic, tested. Her worst fears were confirmed when she was assigned to an intensive signing class. She pictured herself crammed into a tiny first-grader's desk, practicing the alphabet. Suddenly, Joey, who'd been so excited to be where she'd always believed she belonged, began to dread her mother's departure. When Ruth drove away, she would be totally cut off from the hearing and the deaf.

For lunch, she and her mother went to a small restaurant in town, one recommended by the counselor. It was full of returning CSD students. Joey and her mother sat in a booth by the window and watched friends, separated for the summer, jam in together at tables, hands flashing, laughing, and hugging one another. A person from each table, obviously the one with the best oral skills, was sent up to order the sandwiches and act as interpreter for the cashier and the woman behind the counter who took their orders. Joey tried to imagine herself crammed in a booth with a half-dozen friends. How many months, or years, of intensive signing would it take before she would be accepted into a circle of friends?

"Can you tell what they're saying?" her mother asked.

Joey shook her head. "Only a word or two. They're talking too fast."

"For a room full of deaf people, there sure is a lot of noise in here. Why are they pounding on the tables?"

Joey smiled. She could feel the vibrations. "To get each other's attention, Mom."

Ruth shook her head. "I guess I've never really gotten it, have I? You can't hear."

A girl walked by their table and signed HELLO to Joey, then stopped when Joey signed HELLO back. NEW YOU? she asked.

Joey nodded.

WELCOME. MY NAME S-A-R-A-H. NAME YOU?

J-O-E-Y. SIGN NAME J-Y.

NICE MEET YOU. MOTHER YOU?

When Joey nodded, Sarah shook her mother's hand. DEAF YOU? she asked Ruth.

NO, Joey answered. MOTHER HEARING.

NO A-S-L?

Joey shook her head.

GOOD, Sarah signed. WE KEEP SECRETS. She grinned and left to join friends.

Joey looked at her mother. "I just had a whole conversation in sign," she said. "I was getting so scared, but now I think I can do this." She took a sip of Coke, watching Sarah as she squeezed into a booth with friends. *I have to do this,* she thought.

Ruth closed her eyes and let her head drop. She dug in her bag searching for a Kleenex, then used the napkin to dab her eyes and blow her nose. "I can't imagine what I'm going to do without you," she said when she gained control.

"They send us home every weekend. You won't have time to miss me before I'm under foot again."

"I know, but eventually you'll make friends here and spend weekends with their families. Our lives are about to change. . . ." She watched the kids for a moment, then took Joey's hands in hers. "Can you ever forgive me?"

"There's nothing to forgive."

"Oh, sweetheart, I feel like I've done everything wrong since the day you were born."

"No, Mom, you haven't." She squeezed her mother's hand, but couldn't think of what to say to make her feel better.

Another group of kids came in and the hugging started again. "This is where I belong, Mom. Here I won't be different." Joey laughed. "Isn't that wonderful?"

Ruth nodded, but her expression was still sad.

"Mom, what made you change your mind?"

Her mother shrugged. "I'm not sure."

Joey couldn't stop crying as she watched her mother drive

away. She didn't want anyone to see her so she walked to the park down the street from the school. Its manicured lawn was full of Canada geese, hundreds of them. Possibly even Gilbert. The sight of them was almost more than she could bear. She felt so desperately alone as she sat on a swing and cried and cried. Even Sukari was with someone who loved her.

It was nearly sunset when she started back toward school. She stopped once to look back at the geese and wondered how they'd found one another, and how they knew this was where they should be. She remembered how frightened Gilbert had been when Ray put him on the other side of the fence, separate from those he loved but plunked down with others just like himself. Here she was, all alone, trying to fit in where maybe she didn't belong. As the light faded and she walked toward her new life, she suddenly remembered that Gilbert had adjusted. She'd come home from school one day to find a note from her mother: *The man who has Gilbert called to say he is fine. He's still a bit of an outsider on land, eating a little distance from the others, but in the water, they all follow him. As it turns out,* she'd written, *he has the longest neck.* Joey squared her shoulders and smiled, *Long necks run in our family.*

The first letter from her mother came a few days later, along with one from Kenny. His was scrawled on notebook paper and said only that school wasn't the same without her, Kristin had been picked up for shoplifting, and Roxy was back.

The note from her mother was cheery with news of Luke and full of questions about her progress and how she liked her roommate. It ended with the answer to Joey's question of why she'd changed her mind.

It was a long ride home without you and all the way I found my-self wondering why I had decided to let you go. I sure had lots of reasons not to, but none of them held up very well after the party that night. Everyone was having such a good time— except you. On some level, I knew that. Asking you to help me watch Luke was my lame way of trying to include you. Over the years, I've tried to convince myself that you didn't miss what you couldn't hear. I let myself believe that in spite of what you said, you were fully integrated into the family, that you'd do well in school if you tried harder, and that our friends were your friends. When I saw you watching my lips and trying to tap out the rhythm, trying to experience the music, trying to take part in the fun as simple as it was, I felt so ashamed, and then you asked if I was crying over that old song. I had the nerve to tell you that I was crying for all the things I had wanted to do with my life. There you were, fighting daily for the right to make your own choices while I stood in your way and wallowed in self-pity. I've missed what I've missed because I made wrong choices and I was still making wrong choices—for you this time. I've spent the last seven years of your life unable to face the fact of your deafness by ignoring your drive to learn to sign. I believed all along that I was making the right decisions for you, just like I'd believed it was the right choice to marry your father. If I could be that wrong then, maybe I'm wrong now. It breaks my heart to think I may have been robbing you of a fuller life, but to realize that and to continue to do so would be unbearable.

You don't remember how I used to sing to you when you were a baby. Singing is a joyful thing. More than anything, I want you to hear music again, but if that never happens, then at least I want you to have the chance to sing. Learn to sing with your hands, Honey.

All my love, Mom

Joey folded the letter and held it against her heart for a moment before putting it in her pocket. She was learning to sing with her hands. It somehow seemed so appropriate that her life, like the sun, should have changed direction with a summer solstice.

Chapter Eleven

Fourteen months later, November 1993
Fremont, California

Joey closed her eyes against the signing hands of her classmates as they followed Mr. Henderson's interpretation of "Climb Every Mountain" from *The Sound of Music*. She remembered this song, from before she was deaf, being sung by the nuns at the convent. With her eyes shut tight, Joey pictured herself like Julie Andrews, turning slow circles on a golden hilltop, arms open. She didn't see the classroom door open or Mr. Jacobs wave for her attention. Even after someone nudged her and Mr. Henderson signed that she had a phone call, it took a moment for Joey to realize that PHONE YOU was not part of the song.

The TTY was in the office. Joey followed Mr. Jacobs across the courtyard. At the receptionist's desk, she typed, "Joey here," then "GA", which meant "Go Ahead," on the TTY keypad.

"Hi, honey, it's Mom here, GA," appeared slowly, letter by letter, across the narrow screen at the top of the machine.

Joey's stomach lurched. They didn't have a text teletype-writer at home, so her mother, who hated using the message-relay service, never called her. She said it was like having someone listen in on your conversation. On top of that, her mother, Ray, and Luke were coming down for the annual Veterans Day open house. She was sure this call four days before they were to arrive meant bad news. "What's wrong? GA," she typed.

For a moment, there was no response; then, achingly slowly, came her mother's answer: "We're all fine, honey." Another long pause. "It's Sue Carey," the relay operator's misspelling of Sukari.

Joey gripped the edge of the desk, but the next line to come up said, "Can you come home on the afternoon Amtrak? GA."

"Is she dead? GA."

"It's not that. GA."

"What then? GA."

"It will need some explaining," came her mother's cryptic answer.

When the baby across the aisle began to shriek, Joey plucked out the hearing aids—another gift from Charlie—she wore only when she left campus and put them in her coat pocket. The racket reminded her of the temper tantrums Sukari had when she was a baby. She smiled at the young mother trying desperately to quiet her child and wished for the millionth time that she was either totally deaf or not deaf at all. She hated the in-between, where the sound she could hear was an irritation. She put her head back against the coarse fabric of the headrest, closed her eyes, and tried to let the rumble of the bus drown her thoughts. She was exhausted from the dash to get packed, the race to the train station, and then the three-hour wait in Martinez for the bus to Willits, where her mother would pick her up. She was on the final leg and wanted to sleep and not dream, but all she could think about was Sukari and what might have happened to her.

Except for a single visit shortly after Joey started CSD, she and Sukari had been apart for over a year—Joey in Fremont, and Sukari in Fresno with Lynn. Joey'd ridden the train that day, too. From the window she'd seen Lynn sitting trancelike on a bench, unaware that the train was in until Joey touched her arm.

HELLO. WELCOME, Lynn signed. She was hugely pregnant and let Joey help her stand before they hugged.

Lynn, whose sign language skills were still minimal, must have said something when Joey leaned to pick up her bag, because when she stood, Lynn pushed Joey's bushy auburn hair aside to see her ears.

"Sorry, I forgot them," Joey said. She kept her hearing aids in an abalone shell on her desk in the dorm and hadn't given them a thought until that moment.

Lynn crinkled her nose. MY SIGN LANGUAGE, she paused, thinking, then shrugged and said, "is terrible."

"We'll manage," Joey said. "We always did before."

"Sure we will," Lynn said.

Still, aside from Lynn's observation of how happy she looked, they rode to the house in an edgy silence, Lynn maneuvering through traffic, grimly, as if counting the minutes until this visit was over.

Joey forgot her discomfort when she saw Sukari on the back porch riding her tricycle around and around her tire-swing. The sliding glass doors were closed, so Sukari hadn't heard them, and that gave Joey a moment to take in the room.

A huge chain-link cage had been built on the back porch. Joey could see why. The screen was poked out in all the lower corners and there was a long crack in one of the sliding glass doors. The concrete floor was littered with Sukari's toys, and ropes crisscrossed the cage from high corners. Still, it *was* a cage. Joey felt the sting of tears coming, but smiled and glanced at Lynn. The expression on her face was sobering. It reminded Joey of the fatigue and exasperation her mother showed after dealing with Luke all day, but there was more to it than that. Lynn's mouth was touched with bitterness.

Lynn looked at her and tried to smile. "She's a handful."

Sukari suddenly stopped ramming her swing and looked up, then stared at them as if she couldn't believe her eyes.

I-SEE-YOU, Joey signed.

Sukari began to pant-hoot and shake her hands with excitement. The racket she made must have been deafening to Lynn because Joey could hear it faintly herself. She put a finger to her lips.

I-SEE-YOU, J-Y, Sukari signed. COME HUG. HURRY. HURRY.

Lynn opened the sliding glass door and tapped Joey's shoulder. "We had to do this," she said apologetically, then dialed the combination of the padlock.

"I know," Joey said.

Sukari signed, HURRY, HURRY, until the gate swung open,

then she climbed Joey as if she had rungs and wrapped her in powerful, long arms. Joey closed her eyes and buried her face against Sukari's neck, gulping in her musky smell.

"I've missed you," she said, kissing her leathery palms, before stepping into the cage. She moved debris with her foot to clear a corner and sat down. "I brought you a present." Joey pretended to search her pockets.

WANT ME. HURRY, Sukari signed, flailing her hands.

The gift-wrap didn't fool her. She began to food-grunt, an uncontrollable reaction to the sight of food. RAISIN, HURRY.

Joey handed them over.

Sukari ripped the paper and the box, flinging raisins across the floor. After she'd collected a handful and stuffed them into her mouth she signed, RAISIN LOVE ME.

Joey stayed the weekend and Lynn let Sukari sleep in the guest room with her. But on Sunday afternoon, when they began trying to lure her back onto the porch, Sukari got suspicious and refused to go near it. Out of desperation, they borrowed the neighbor's dog to scare her into her cage.

Even after six months, Joey still cried over the memory of Sukari clutching the chain-link wall, yanking on it with her hands and feet and screaming as Joey, tears streaming down her face, walked out the door.

For a while after that Lynn wrote breezy notes about Sukari's antics, but after the birth of her daughter, those stopped.

The bus driver reached across the aisle and tapped her knee. "Willits," he said.

Joey sat up and rubbed her eyes. She was glad she'd worn her new red sweatshirt with DEAF PRIDE embossed across her chest, because she'd fallen asleep without remembering to tell him she couldn't hear the towns when he called them out. "Thanks." She yawned.

"Is she here for you?" he asked, exaggerating the words and pointing toward her tired-looking mother at the curb.

"Yes, sir." Joey waved.

"Am I glad to see you." Ruth folded Joey into her arms before she was fully off the bus. A rear door of her mother's Ford Explorer swung open. Luke scrambled out and ran into her arms.

"How's school?" Joey asked him. "Can you add yet?"

"One plus one is two," Luke shouted. "Two plus two is four." Her mother covered his mouth with her hand.

Joey hitched him under her arm and carried him to the car.

"Sit with me," Luke shouted.

"No, we want to talk," Ruth said.

"Bummer." Luke snapped his fingers.

Ruth rolled her eyes. "I'm afraid this is only the beginning. He comes home from kindergarten with a new expression every day. How's Michelle?"

Michelle was Joey's roommate, and it was her family with whom Joey lived on weekends. What started as a once-a-month treat from having to travel all the way to Fort Bragg and back each weekend had become a permanent arrangement when Joey proved to be the more trustworthy babysitter for Michelle's little sister. "She's in love."

"Who this week?"

Joey laughed. "I don't bother with their names anymore. It'll be really scary when her mother actually lets her date."

"Don't think I haven't thought of that. She's so boy-crazy."

Joey knew she shouldn't tell her mother about Michelle, but she felt compelled. Being open about her roommate might reassure her mother that she had better sense. At sixteen, Joey was six months older than her mother had been when she fell in love with her father.

They passed the old Willits barn. Three miles of small talk was enough. "So tell me about Sukari," Joey said.

"Not now. The road's too twisty," Ruth answered.

Route 20 was thirty-three miles of curves. It was the shortest way to the coast across the stretch where the two North Coast ranges shouldered each other, but it was not a piece of road to take your eyes off. "You're right." Joey turned to talk to Luke but he was hypnotized by his Pac-Man game, leaving Joey to stare out the window, lost in memories of Sukari.

Ray came out of the house and waved as they pulled in. HOW SCHOOL? he signed, then grinned. RIGHT?

Joey laughed. YES. RIGHT. "School's fine. School's great. You're really clicking along."

Ruth tapped her shoulder. "He's about a quarter of the way through the book Charlie gave you, and Luke's got the whole alphabet and a few words under his belt."

"Oh, Ray, that's so nice of you."

WANT US TALK, he signed.

Joey hugged him, quickly, then turned to take her overnight bag from the backseat. That's when she saw a familiar car parked under the fir tree.

"What's Lynn . . . ?" She looked toward the house.

Lynn stood at the window, holding her baby, whose hand she lifted and waved at Joey.

The hand Joey lifted in return trembled. She turned to Ruth. "You said she wasn't dead. Is Sukari dead?"

"She's not, honey. I promise."

Ruth set their meeting up like a conference on the deck off the upstairs bedroom. There was a notepad for Lynn to write on and glasses filled with iced tea and an ominous box of tissues.

As much as she loved babies, Joey couldn't even pretend interest in little Katie. She could think only of Sukari as she faced Lynn and her mother. If Sukari wasn't dead, how much worse could it be that Lynn had felt obliged to drive up here, probably passing Joey's bus on the way?

Lynn stuck a pacifier in Katie's mouth, and sat down, heaving a sigh so heavy that her long bangs fluttered. The look she gave Ruth was full of resignation and something else that it took Joey a second to recognize as thinly veiled hostility. Not at all what she'd expected. For some reason, she had assumed that they were in this together. Why she thought that, she didn't know. Perhaps because they were adults, who seemed to enter into conspiracies against kids even when they didn't like each other.

The day was bright and sunny. An Anna's hummingbird dived in and hovered near the baby's red cap, then zipped away. If the scene had been caught in a photograph it would be one of those shiny-postcard moments.

Ruth held a letter out, which Joey took. The return address was Lynn's and the postmark was four months old. It was still sealed but Joey was sure that her mother had either read it or knew what it was about. Why else would she have kept it from Joey? And was this the reason Lynn seemed hostile toward her mother?

Lynn avoided looking at her and reached instead to shift the baby so that she was sitting in a pool of sunlight. Her face, for that moment, was filled with affection, very different from how Joey remembered her with Sukari during her Fresno visit. With a sick feeling in her stomach, she got up and took her letter to the creek side of the deck. It opened easily.

Dear Joey, I am so sorry to have to tell you this, and I want you to know that I did everything I could to avoid it, but we had to give Sukari to a zoo.

After hours of dread, relief swept over her. A zoo. That was okay. It wasn't what she would have wanted for Sukari but she'd been on a field trip to the Oakland Zoo and seen the chimps there. They'd seemed happy, chasing each other, swinging on ropes, and spinning in tires. She'd much prefer to see Sukari there than on Lynn's cramped little porch. Joey looked up, almost smiling, but the expressions on their faces frightened her again. Her fingers tightened on the thin paper in her hands as she read on.

When I came home from the hospital, I wanted Sukari to understand that Katie was a permanent addition. I began by nursing her in a rocking chair near Sukari's cage so she could watch. I even moved close enough for her to poke a finger through the wire and touch the baby's cheek. I thought including her would keep her from becoming jealous.

I suppose, without knowing any better, I made things worse. I put Katie's bassinet in the living room so Sukari could see that she lived with us. Unfortunately, Sukari got so attached to her that if the baby cried, she would go nuts in her cage, banging and throwing her toys. Her devotion to Katie was scary and the racket was awful unless the baby was right where she could see her, day and night.

The final straw was all my fault. I had just given Sukari her lunch when the phone rang. The baby was asleep and I ran to answer it and didn't get the padlock locked tightly. She got out and took Katie from her crib. When I found them, Sukari had her up on her bed-board, six feet off the ground, and, bless her heart, was trying to nurse her. When I tried to get the baby away from her, she swung off the platform, ended up dangling by one hand from the wire roof of the cage, with Katie draped over her arm, the way she used to carry Hidey. I was terrified that she would drop her, though never afraid that she would hurt her intentionally. Charlie always said she'd sell her soul for raisins. I gave her two boxes to engage both hands so she had to put Katie down.

I keep telling myself she will be better off with her own kind. And that she'll become a mother herself someday. And I pray Charlie will forgive me, and that you will.

Lynn

Lynn had been writing on the pad as Joey finished the letter. "So she *is* in a zoo?"

Neither of them answered. When Ruth looked at Lynn, waiting for her to finish, Joey knew there was more news, and that it wasn't good. She closed her eyes. A chill swept over her as if a wind had come up. She began to shiver.

"You need a sweater," Ruth said. She got up and went into her bedroom and came back with a sweatshirt for Joey.

When Joey finished pulling it over her head, she saw they'd said something that she'd missed and that Lynn, by the set of her jaw, was angry. She turned away and tucked Katie's blanket around her more snugly, then sat up and tried to smile. She took Joey's hand and held it tightly before sliding the pad across the table.

There's no way to soften this. Sukari didn't do well at the zoo. They told me that chimps that are raised by humans never accept themselves as chimpanzees, but I had hoped Sukari would be the exception. Instead she was as terrified of them as she is of dogs. She called them "black bugs."

The staff eventually moved her to a cage by herself, but I think the isolation was worse. She spent the days rocking and signing to herself as if she'd lost her mind.

Joey pulled her hand free and flipped the page.

Lynn scooped Katie up and hugged her.

They didn't have the facilities nor the funds, nor the inclination, I suspect, to keep her isolated. When they were sure that she would never adjust, they said I had to take her back or find a rehab facility that would accept her.

Lynn rested her chin on the top of the baby's head. Tears rolled down her cheeks and dropped to form silver beads on Katie's red wool cap.

I called all over trying to find a place, but there are hundreds of chimps in need of a place to go, and they were especially uninterested in a chimp who can't be housed with other chimps.

Joey, shortly after Sukari went to the zoo, I went back to work and hired a full-time, live-in nanny to care for Katie. We've turned the porch into a sunroom. Even if I wanted to, we couldn't have taken Sukari back. Last month, she was sent to a facility in Norman, Oklahoma. It's a kind of clearinghouse for unwanted chimpanzees. Most eventually go to research labs.

The note ended there. Joey looked up, tears brimming in her eyes. "Where is she?"

Lynn bit her lip, took a deep breath, then handed Joey a letter.

Dear Dr. Mansell: In response to your query, dated October 10, our records show that chimpanzee #1029, formerly known as Sukari, has been sent to the Clarke Foundation in Alamogordo, New Mexico. She will be used in their pesticide testing program. If you require further . . .

Joey closed her eyes and swallowed over and over, trying not to throw up. She staggered to her feet, knocking the chair over and scaring Katie, who began to wail. The leg of the chair tripped her and she stumbled but batted her mother away when she tried to help her up. When she got her footing, she lurched across the bedroom and out the door to the carport. She ran the trail toward Charlie's, beating her way through the ferns and huckleberries that grabbed at her legs. The tree that had toppled during the earthquake was still across the trail. She climbed over it and stepped into the icy stream. She ran with the rush of the creek. The next tree to block her path was Charlie's alder, covered with oyster mushrooms, fresh and abundant. She stopped when she saw them and looked up at his house. "Charlie," she cried.

The woman who was sitting on the deck got up, came to the railing, and looked down at her. She shouted something. Joey saw her hands frame her mouth, before she turned and called to someone in the house. A man came out, ran down the steps and down the trail toward her.

Joey dropped to the bank and folded over her knees, sobbing with the smell of mud and pine needles in her nose. Her heart burned like a broken blister.

When the man tried to lift her, Joey jerked free and crawled away. He grabbed her and wrapped his arms around her and held tightly until she began to shiver.

The woman came with a blanket and together they helped Joey up the hill toward the house. About halfway up, they met her mother, Lynn, and the baby, coming down.

At the bottom of the steps, Joey looked up. The sunlight played with the wind-stirred shadows on the deck, rolling and flickering. She squinted, praying for one small shadow to scramble toward her, and for the sun to light the white hair of an old man. But the jungle gym was gone, French doors replaced the sliding glass ones, and the house had been painted beige with trim the color of dried blood. She couldn't remember what color it had been. She sank down to sit on the bottom step. Her mother sat with her and held her while she cried. The couple who lived in Charlie's house went inside and closed their doors.

It was dark out when she woke, and for a moment Joey hoped it had all been a nightmare and now it was over. She knew it wasn't; everything Charlie had feared for Sukari had come true. She remembered Ruth and Lynn driving her home and that they'd been openly mad at each other when they helped her into the house and into her room. Lynn sat on the edge of the bed, smoothing her hair, but when she tried to tell her something, Ruth stepped in, saying that it could wait. Joey didn't fight back. She didn't think she could stand more details.

She'd sobbed herself into total numbness, pretending to be asleep when her mother came to cover her with a blanket. She wasn't sure how long she'd lain there, trying not to imagine the horrors Sukari was suffering, before she really did fall asleep.

Joey rolled over and looked at her clock. It was after one. She got up and, with her hands jammed in her armpits for warmth, went out and into the bathroom. She pressed a wet, cold washcloth against her swollen eyes for a few minutes, then brushed her teeth, wondering all the time what it was her mother was keeping from her. Maybe Sukari had already died, and Ruth was saving that news for after Joey adjusted to this loss.

When Lynn came by early the next morning to say goodbye, Ray insisted she stay for breakfast, but she came in only for coffee and didn't stay long enough to finish a full cup. Outside, with Ruth making an obvious effort to ensure that she and Joey weren't alone together, she turned from strapping Katie into her car seat and took Joey's hands, pressing something into one of her palms. "There's still hope. Don't think that this is over." Lynn hugged her, looked at Ruth, got into the car, and drove up the driveway.

Joey jammed her hands into her pockets. A few minutes later, in the bathroom, she read the note: *Remember what Charlie said. She's yours. Call Bryan McCully.*

Chapter Twelve

Joey arrived back at school late Sunday afternoon. First thing Monday morning, she went to the office and used the TTY to call Mr. McCully's office. His secretary took the message. He was in Los Angeles, trying a case, and wouldn't be back for at least a week.

For the next few days she went from class to class, meal to meal in a daze. The weekend came, and though she loved football, she begged off going to the game with Michelle and Jenny, claiming to have cramps and a raging headache. She needed to be alone, away from Michelle's buoyancy and the spirited pre-game enthusiasm.

Every afternoon, after classes, she walked to the park where she'd seen the geese that first day. She sat in the same swing each time, walked it forward, then let her own weight drag her backward over and over until she had created trenches in the sand with her heels. Joey tried not to think about Sukari's circumstances, but her imagination ran unchecked: a small cage, someone spraying her in the face with Raid, or giving her toxic shots.

As hard as she tried to escape those thoughts by focusing on what she would say to Mr. McCully when he returned her call, she couldn't. The only plan she'd come up with was to use her college funds to buy Sukari back. But even if that worked, where could she go with a half-grown chimpanzee? The more she thought about it, the more hopeless she believed it was. By the weekend, she felt herself giving up and growing toward trying to accept Sukari's death.

In history class on the following Tuesday, an aide from the office came to tell her there was a call for her.

With trembling fingers, she typed, "Joey Willis here, GA."

"Joey, this is Mr. McCully. My secretary said you called. There was also a call from Lynn telling me about Sukari. GA."

"I've been trying to figure out a way to get her back and was hoping maybe we could use the money Charlie left me for college to buy her back. GA."

"I think we can do better than that. Can you come into San Francisco this Saturday? GA."

"Yes, sir. GA."

"Shall I send a car for you? GA."

Joey wanted to say yes, but a car showing up for her would generate questions and require permission from her mother. "I can take a bus. GA."

"I have another appointment at noon, so can we meet for breakfast at the Hyatt on Union Square? GA."

Joey had never been to a fancy restaurant. "What should I wear? GA."

"Your very best jeans and your thinking cap."

Thinking cap?

On Friday afternoon, Joey told Michelle that she was going home for the weekend to babysit for Luke. Without a clue where she would spend Saturday night, Joey caught the 6:30 A.M. bus to San Francisco.

Though Joey had seen the San Francisco skyline many times from the Oakland side of the bay on her trips home, the size of it up close was beyond imagination. She came out of the dark, low-ceilinged terminal into a sleeping giant of a city where the early morning sun made the windows of skyscrapers glow like hot coals. There was little traffic and fewer people. Even the homeless still slept in doorways and alcoves.

Joey leaned against the outside wall of the terminal and stared at the city. When she'd come through the station, all the ticket windows had been closed and she had no idea how to find her way to the Hyatt. She went back inside to check the walls for a map or to ask someone for directions.

A homeless man in a wheelchair was setting up his begging station at one of the entrances. He'd placed an open guitar case on the floor, but she saw no guitar. He glanced at Joey, but his shaggy beard covered his mouth. She smiled shyly and walked on.

Inside, in a dark corner beneath a staircase, an old man sat surrounded by newspapers and magazines. He watched her come across the marble floor through veiled, angry-looking eyes. Just as she stopped, he suddenly glanced to his right. Joey looked where he looked. The rackety metal Gray Line tour window was just going up. By the time Joey reached it, another person, who had materialized from nowhere, had gotten there ahead of her.

When she stepped to the window, the clerk smiled at her.

Joey returned her smile and was comforted. "I'm deaf," she said. "Could you show me how to get to the Hyatt on Union Square?"

"Oh, I'm so sorry. Sure." The woman shuffled some papers, found a red pen, then reached through the window and took a map from the display rack that she'd just placed there. She outlined the little blue Gray Line triangular logo, which was inside a shaded square labeled TRANSBAY TERMINAL.

Joey smiled. Most people were awfully nice.

She added a "you are here" arrow. Next, she studied the map herself, located Union Square, then drew a rectangle in the blank area on its north side and cross-hatched it with red lines. *Hyatt,* she wrote and drew another arrow. She showed Joey, who smiled, said thank you, and reached for it. Four people were in line behind her.

"No, wait." The woman opened a drawer and found a green pen. Carefully, so as not to cover the names of the streets, she traced the route Joey should take.

Is this clear? she wrote along the margin.

"Very clear," Joey said. "Thank you."

Joey was nearly to the entrance when the woman caught up and tapped her shoulder. She'd scrawled, **Let me get you a cab,** on an envelope. She tried to hand Joey five dollars.

"Is it that far?"

5 or 6 blocks.

Joey gently pushed the money away. "No, thank you. I can walk and I'm hours early."

Joey slung her backpack over one shoulder but by the time

she got to the first corner, she decided that wearing it was safer. There still weren't many people out: one jogger, a couple of people walking dogs, and a few homeless men.

She had quarters in her pocket left over from the bus fare. The first homeless man she passed had a sign that read, HOME-LESS VET, PLEASE HELP IF U CAN. She put a quarter on his blanket. He didn't look up. She understood why. So far, nothing had wiped from her memory the looks people had given them during those weeks before the restaurant hired her mother. Joey also remembered that it was the other homeless who had kept them fed.

On the sidewalk outside Macy's, across the park from the Hyatt, Joey gave her last two quarters to a man who was breaking the sausage and cheese part of a McMuffin into bite-size pieces for his red-sweater-wearing cat while he ate the bread.

She found the Plaza Restaurant on the first floor of the Hyatt but decided to wait outside when she saw a uniformed man watching her. She got the creepy feeling that if she went inside and sat down, the Hyatt man would ask her to leave.

Outside on the steps, she examined a fountain created from a jumble of raised copper-plated scenes of San Francisco landmarks. She settled on the top step near the one of the Golden Gate Bridge to watch for Mr. McCully.

It wasn't long before she saw him bound up the steps, but he went straight into the restaurant and was looking for her when she touched his arm.

HELLO. He shook her hand. SORRY LATE. NICE SEE-YOU AGAIN.

THANK YOU. NICE MEET-YOU AGAIN.

The dining room looked full, but the hostess led them through the maze of tables to one by the window overlooking Union Square. There was a Reserved sign on it, which she removed as Mr. McCully pulled Joey's chair out for her. The hostess took Joey's napkin from the table, snapped it open, and let it float to cover her knees. "Enjoy your breakfast," she said, handing her a leather-bound menu. From the window Joey could see the red-sweatered cat curled and asleep beside his friend.

"Are you wearing your hearing aids?" Mr. McCully asked.

They were in her pocket. She shook her head. "They don't work in crowded places. They amplify all the sounds so I only end up hearing racket."

Mr. McCully patted her hand. "How well do you read lips?"

"Depends. Some people's are easier than others. But if I catch a few words, I can sometimes guess the rest."

Mr. McCully took a long yellow pad and a pen from his briefcase. *I don't sign all that well, so we'll make do with reading and writing instead of signs and lip-reading, if that's okay with you.*

Joey nodded.

"Do you want to eat first?"

"Is there hope for Sukari?"

"Yes."

"I'd rather know that first."

GOOD. *I have something for you to read.* From his briefcase he took a fat, maroon leather notebook. ESTATE PLANNING PORTFOLIO was embossed in gold letters across its middle. He

opened it to a page he'd marked with a yellow Post-it, opened the
rings, and took out a few pages. THE LAST WILL OF DR. CHARLES
WILLIAM MCKINLEY MANSELL was the title of the first page.

Mr. McCully laid the will between them, then wrote, *Your
mother told Lynn that Charlie signed something to you
just before he died.*

"She's yours," Joey said, signing, SHE YOURS, for him to see.

He meant just that. Mr. McCully opened the will, flipped
a few pages, pointed to the third paragraph, and turned the
document for Joey to read.

> *All decisions concerning issues of care, maintenance,*
> *housing and well-being for the aforementioned chim-*
> *panzee, Sukari, will be decided by and at the sole*
> *discretion of her guardian, Joanne Elizabeth Willis,*
> *aka Joey.*

An odd taste rose in Joey's throat. Bile. She knew it from the
many times she'd thrown up as a child. She reached for her
water glass and drank in great, long gulps.

"She was mine. All along, she was mine? Why didn't anybody tell me?" Tears of anger welled in her eyes.

As if he'd guessed this would be her response, he'd already
written, *Your mother didn't want us to tell you about this
part of the will. Charlie also left a trust fund for Sukari, but
unfortunately, the way it's set up, you are her sole guardian
and the money to take care of her is funded at your dis-
cretion. No one's been able to access it to help Sukari.*

"My mother knew about this?"

She must have raised her voice, because Mr. McCully glanced around, patted her hand, then quickly wrote, *She knows Charlie left Sukari's fate in your hands. I don't think she knows about the trust fund. She never saw the will or wanted to discuss it.*

"Did I have the right to decide what happened to her?"

"Yes."

"Have I always had that right, even though I'm young?"

"Yes."

"Why did Lynn let the zoo have her? And why did she let the zoo give her away? I don't understand this."

Mr. McCully reached across and took her hand in both of his. People had turned and were looking at them. The hostess started across the room but Mr. McCully waved her off.

Joey realized she was crying only when he handed her his handkerchief. She wiped her eyes. "Can we get her back?"

"Yes," he said.

Joey stared at his lips. Had he really said yes?

YES, he signed, then scrawled another sentence and handed it to her: *I have already filed an injunction to stop any further testing on her and a copy of the will has been sent to the Clarke Foundation's attorneys.*

When Joey looked up, he took the pad and wrote, *The hitch is we have no one willing to house her.*

"What do you mean?" she asked before she realized that she already knew the answer. If the zoo wouldn't keep her and Lynn couldn't and her mother wouldn't, where else was left? She didn't bother to read his answer. "Can we pay some place to keep her for a while?"

*Possibly. Lynn thought of that but it costs thousands a
year to feed and care for a chimpanzee. She didn't have
that kind of money. As long as Lynn thought Sukari was
okay in the zoo, she abided by your mother's wishes. But
now . . . well, the situation has changed.*

"Can we try again?"

*I called some zoos. Not one wanted another chim-
panzee. They are overwhelmed by the numbers needing a
place to go. They keep the ones they have on birth control.*

Joey remembered something Lynn had said about rehab
places. At the time, it had had another association for her: Her
father had been sent to one for alcoholics. He'd walked out after two days. "Lynn mentioned calling rehab places. What are
they?"

*They are permanent homes for animals nobody wants.
Circus animals. Movie animals. Air Force chimps. Research facility survivors. Lynn tried them all, I think. No
room there either.*

"Do you know why I'm deaf?"

The question seemed to catch him off guard. "No. No, I
don't."

"My father beat me." She'd never said the words out loud before and was surprised at how easily they came. "If my mother
had left him the first time he hit her, I wouldn't be deaf."

Slowly, thoughtfully, Mr. McCully wrote, *It can be almost
as dangerous to leave an abuser as it is to stay. It requires
a lot of courage to make a run for it.*

"Well, she's definitely not brave. And she never cared much

for Sukari, but she knew that I did, Mr. McCully. She knows I
love her. I think she owed it to me not to let this happen."

After breakfast, Mr. McCully told Joey he had a few minutes before he had to leave for his next meeting and asked if
she'd like to see the city from the roof of the Hyatt.

The elevator opened onto a large room on the thirty-sixth
floor. There was a bar, a dance floor, tables and chairs, and a
bank of windows, from knee-high to the ceiling, with a spec-
tacular view. Perhaps, on any other day, she would have appreciated him taking the time to bring her here. But right now,
she didn't have the heart to enjoy the view of cable cars, like
miniatures, creeping up and down Powell Street, the colorful,
curly gates of Chinatown, and the bay dotted with little white
sailboats. She nodded politely and tried to smile when he
pointed out Alcatraz on its barren rock, the fire-hose, nozzle-
shaped Coit Tower, and the pointy-topped TransAmerica Building, writing their names for her in the condensation on the
windows.

I have to go, he wrote. *I'm happy to give you a ride back
to the station, but I have one more thing for you and I
thought perhaps you'd like some time alone.*

What else? she thought. She did want to be alone, she was
sure of that. "I'd like to stay, if it's okay."

Mr. McCully squeezed her shoulder and nodded, then took
an envelope from his inside coat pocket. "This is for you." It
was addressed to her in Charlie's shaky handwriting and dated
September 29th, a little over a month after Sukari's and Joey's
birthday party.

Joey waved as Mr. McCully stepped into the elevator, then took her letter to a chair by the window.

Dearest Joey. I write this letter to you today but hope it will be years before you read it. Still, my health is failing so I don't think I should wait much longer. When you do read this, I will be gone, or worse, no longer capable of making essential decisions. I am therefore placing a huge responsibility on your young shoulders. After I learned that Lynn was to marry Jack, I decided that it should be you who determines Sukari's fate. Lynn will want to have children and though she loves Sukari, her own children will, of course, become her first priority. You will marry, too, someday, but by then you will have settled Sukari into a permanent arrangement.

Bryan will explain all the details to you. And you can say no. Nothing I am doing for you hinges on your accepting responsibility for her. But without your voice to protect her, I'm afraid of what might happen. Every day I am reminded that we have to be taught to be human, each of us in our turn. Other animals know what it is to be what they are. A cat knows what it is to be a cat, a dog a dog, a chimp a chimp. But Sukari has learned, better than some people, what it is to be human and for that I may not be forgiven. Without your guardianship, and perhaps intervention on her behalf, I fear whatever her future holds may be more dreadful for the fact of her understanding her condition.

I did not ask your mother's permission; I knew what her answer would be. Hopefully, you will be much older than you are now when our fates befall us. I look forward to watching you grow strong and wise, but if you are reading this sooner rather than later, then let me tell you that my greatest regret will be having missed watching you become a woman. You are the grandchild I never had. I believe we were meant to meet that day by the creek. I'll never know why this mean old man went unpunished, receiving instead a treasure. For Sukari and me, you were heaven-sent. I love you both terribly.

Charlie

Joey looked up from the letter and into the damp eyes of her reflection in the window. "Oh, Charlie, you shouldn't have left this job to me." She covered her face with her hands. "I don't know what to do," she sobbed.

A light mist was falling by the time she stood to go, soundless even to the hearing, with drops so small and fine that, at home, it turned spider webs into nets of diamonds. She put her forehead against the cold glass, nose to nose with the fuzzy image of her face. She swiped at her eyes with the heel of her hand and stared down at the ant-people. From thirty-six floors above the street she could see how puny and powerless humans really were: little squashable dots. She put her head back. Was Charlie up there, watching her now, and did he regret what he'd done? She thought suddenly of the song they'd been signing when her mother's phone call came: "Climb Every Mountain." She began to sign it to herself, then closed her eyes. In class, she'd remembered the music, but here she could conjure up only the image of Julie Andrews spinning in the sunlight on a green mountaintop. She looked out the mist-coated windows at the blurry city beyond. It seemed so important for her to re-member. If she could, it might help her to know what to do. Instead, tears erupted and spilled down her cheeks.

By the time Joey came out of the Hyatt, the mist had turned into a heavy fog, her stepfather's definition of a light drizzle. The homeless man and his cat were gone, and she caught her-self worrying about where.

She looked up at the hotel and the surrounding forest of skyscrapers, many with their top floors invisible in the mist. If she'd felt hopeless up there, down here, on the crowded street, with a lid of fog over the city, she felt doomed to fail.

For a while, she walked aimlessly, trying to decide what to do and where to go. She couldn't go back to school, and she didn't want to go to Michelle's. Her only choice was to go home, but she wasn't ready to do that, either.

The streets were crowded with people shopping for Christ-mas. She'd forgotten how close the holidays were: Thanksgiv-ing was less than two weeks away.

For as long as she could remember, Joey had felt sad around the holidays—a dark moodiness usually reserved for adults. She and her mother had talked about it once. Ruth said it was because losses are remembered more vividly in seasons of so-called joy, and adults usually have more of them to count than young people do. Joey stood facing the brightly lit windows of Casual Corner, with its racks of colorful clothes, and tried to remember Smiley's face.

The last time she'd seen her she was standing in the blowing snow, signing I-LOVE-YOU as her mother pulled away from the hospital, headed for their new life in Fort Bragg. Smiley had thrown Joey a combination Thanksgiving, Christmas, and birthday party on the day she left. She reached and traced one of the scars behind her ears, looking again at her reflection in the glass. That's when she noticed a scruffy-looking man watching her from the other side of the street. Joey hurried away.

She'd gone a block or two when her skin began to prickle. She glanced sideways. The man, stoop-shouldered, dirty, and bearded, had caught up with her and was walking so close to her left elbow that her jacket sleeve brushed his arm. She jumped aside. His mouth moved and a palm-up hand wriggled like a dying roach in the space between them. She smelled the reek of his whiskey-breath and the filthy-ashtray stink of his fingers.

Joey jammed her hands into her pockets looking for quarters, then remembered she'd given them all away. He pressed closer. Joey gasped as if he'd grabbed her and turned sharply right into the path of another man, who squeezed her arm as he maneuvered around her. She stepped off the curb. Brakes squealed and a horn blasted. She jumped back. The driver shouted, "You idiot," and zoomed away. She smelled the man again and felt her backpack pressed against his chest.

Joey swallowed and ran to the corner where one sign said DON'T WALK and the other flashed DON'T WALK. She stepped in front of a woman, putting her between the man and herself. The woman gave her a dirty look and pushed past Joey when the light changed.

Joey ran across the street. At the curb, she glanced back. The man was crossing slowly, sloppily. She felt like a mouse on one of those wheels in a cage. Her chest tightened and it was hard to catch her breath, but even in the cold, her underarms were wet with perspiration.

WALK flashed on the other corner. Joey darted across the intersection. She heard a horn blast and looked to see the man with his hand on the hood of a car. The driver honked again and shook a fist, but the man ignored the gesture and started after her again.

She ran toward the next intersection, where DON'T WALK flashed red. "Run," her mother screamed, blood streaming from where the kitchen stool had split her eyebrow in half. She saw her father turn his fiery red eyes on her. "Run, Joey. Run," her mother screamed again. She did, out the trailer door, past her father's car with the door still open, the keys in the ignition, dinging. She crouched behind the car. He stood on the top step looking for her. When she peeked over the trunk, he saw her. "I'm going to fix you this time," he roared. Her mother had his ankle. When he turned to kick her off, Joey ran for the woodshed, scrunched into a dark corner, and watched the shadow coming for her, swelling to blot out the light, then the stool leg coming down.

Someone bumped her. She screamed and raised her arms to protect her head. Nothing happened. No crushing pain. No darkness. She smelled exhaust fumes, not pine and cedar. She looked around. There were people everywhere. Passing silently, staring.

She walked, her heart still thumping crazily in her chest, to a windowsill outside a restaurant and sat down. The drizzle had covered her with a misty coating that looked almost metallic. She gulped air until her heart slowed, then she took her map and marker from her backpack. She circled Mason and O'Farrell, the corner where she was, in blue, then traced the most direct route to the red square that marked the bus terminal.

A pair of legs in dirty, ratty jeans stopped in front of her, close enough for the map to brush his pants legs. His stale, oily odor almost gagged her. When she looked up, he said, "Boo," in a burst of whiskey breath.

Joey felt as if she were shrinking, like in the old movie where a man shriveled until he was forced to fight a spider with a straight pin. She pulled her head down between her shoulders and closed her eyes. Her mother, her forehead split and bleeding, her arm up to protect herself from another blow, kicked out at the legs standing over her. Joey wanted to bite one again, to feel the lump of flesh between her teeth, and hear her father howl, but she couldn't move. Instead, she waited for the smell of cut, dry firewood, and the darkness that always ended this nightmare.

The stink of whiskey and stale cigarettes grew stronger. She grimaced, waiting for the sharp pain. When it didn't come, she opened her eyes. The man leaned over her, one hand splayed against the window above her head for support, his face close to hers. He tapped her map. "Are you lost?"

She dodged under his arm. "Leave me alone."

He laughed.

For the first time, she saw his eyes. They were a watery blue with red rims and dilated pupils. There was no rage in them. He was in his thirties, she guessed, but he hadn't been young for a long time, and his beard was only a couple of weeks old, probably grown since his last bath. He was her height. "You look like my father," she said.

The man blinked.

Joey didn't. "I can't hear you because I'm deaf. He made me deaf."

Two people stopped, so Joey knew she'd said that out loud.

"I'm not afraid of you. You can't hurt me."

The man shrank back and glanced at the people stopping. A woman took a phone from her briefcase and held it for the man to see as she punched in 911.

The small, bent stick of a man scuttled away, looking over his shoulder and shaking a yellow fist once before turning the corner.

The woman put her phone away. DEAF YOU?

Joey nodded.

SEE M-A-P. LOST YOU?

"I was just getting my bearings. I'm headed for the bus terminal."

NOT FAR. ME WALK WITH YOU?

"No, ma'am. I'm fine now. How do you know sign language?"

SISTER DEAF. WALK WITH YOU, ME.

Joey shook her head. "I'm okay now. Really. I was scared, but not anymore. Thank you."

She struck off down the street with a lighter step, as if the entire population of San Francisco had been lifted off her shoulders—with a single exception. Near the Hyatt, she stopped and looked up at the top-floor windows. "I *can* do this, Charlie," she whispered.

Chapter Thirteen

The woman who had drawn the map for her was still at the Gray Line window. "Hi," she said, then got a concerned look on her face. "Did you find the Hyatt?"

"Yes, thank you. Would you do me another favor?"

"Sure."

"Please call my mother and tell her to meet the four-thirty Greyhound in Willits." Joey handed her the number. "Call collect. She'll accept," she added, then thanked her and walked away. Joey could have made the call herself, through the relay operator, but she didn't want to talk to her mother; she wanted her to worry and fret for the next four hours.

Even though they arrived late, the ride was not long enough for Joey. When she saw her mother's car parked near the bus stop and the tip of her cigarette glowing in the dark, all the anger she'd tried to reason away on the trip returned to bang like a drum in her head.

"Are you all right? Are you sick?" Her mother reached to feel her forehead when Joey got into the car.

Joey pulled away.

"What's wrong?"

"I don't want to talk about it here."

Her mother started the engine. "There better be a good excuse for this." She turned off the interior light and reached for the gearshift.

Joey clamped her wrist. "I went to see Mr. McCully today, Mom. I hope your excuse is a good one, too."

Ruth smacked the steering wheel with one hand, then drove off.

Poor Hidey. Luke had taken over where Sukari had left off. When Joey came in, he was pushing the cat around the room in a wicker laundry basket.

After hugging Luke, Joey picked Hidey up and buried her nose in his fur. He used to carry traces of Sukari's smell but now the odor was of the rich pine-needle duff of his cushy hiding place in the woods. He rubbed the sides of his face against her chin over and over and began to rumble against her chest.

When her mother brushed past her and headed for the kitchen, Joey tensed for the fight that was coming because she wasn't going to let her mother avoid it. For Sukari's sake, she couldn't. Every minute counted. "Where do you want to go to talk about this, Mom?"

"No place. Dinner's late," she said, "and Ray's on his way home. Tomorrow will be soon enough."

"Soon enough for whom?"

"He had no right to call you."

"I called him, Mom. And you're the one who had no right here. I don't understand how you could let something I love as much as I love Sukari be sent to a place like that."

Luke wanted something and her mother opened the refrigerator, blocking Joey's view of whatever she answered, if she'd answered at all. With her back to Joey, she poured him a glass of milk and gave him an Oreo.

"Did you answer me, Mom?"

Ruth turned. "I know you love her, but she's not like the cat. She's as big a handful as ten Lukes."

Her milk-mustached brother looked up and grinned.

"We couldn't keep her."

"No one asked you to. But if I'd known about the will, I could have kept them from sending her to that place. It's the worst one. Mr. McCully said so."

"Now, Joey. They have all sorts of humane guidelines for those places."

"What do you know about them?" Joey cried. "How humane can they be to take an animal, any animal, but especially Sukari, who's known one kind of life, and shut her in a cage and poison her? What guidelines do they have for that, Mom? What could they possibly do to make that okay?"

"You're shouting." Ruth arched her scarred eyebrow and shook a finger at her. "Don't use that tone of voice with me."

"Tone? I'm not allowed to be angry?"

"I did what I thought was best. We couldn't take her. I thought she'd have a good home with Lynn."

"But when she didn't have a good home, why didn't you tell me?"

"I just thought it would hurt you. I mean, what could we do? They should have put her to sleep."

"She's still a baby, not an old sick dog."

"Joey, you're not being fair to me."

"Fair to you? Being fair to you is not at the top of my list right now, Mom."

"Why did he leave the responsibility for her up to you, anyway? A child."

"He didn't plan to die as soon as he did."

"Well, still."

"Sukari trusted me, don't you see? That's the really bad part. She only had me to count on."

Her mother's head snapped back as if Joey had struck her. She turned to put Luke's glass in the sink, but missed. It shattered against the edge of the counter, slicing her finger. Blood dripped onto the floor, unnoticed by her mother. "You're twisting this around and making it about me and your father."

"You're the one doing the twisting. This isn't about what you did or didn't do for me. It's about . . ." Joey stopped, realizing that she did believe it was the same, and recognized that the anger she harbored had just been ripped from somewhere deep inside and now lay raw and exposed between them.

Joey stared at the bloody puddle growing at her mother's feet. "You're bleeding."

Ruth looked down, then back at Joey in surprise, as if the blood were from the wound Joey had just then inflicted. She reached blindly for the dishtowel and wrapped it around her hand. "You've never forgiven me, have you?" Tears welled.

"Forgiven what?" Luke asked. He was sitting on the counter watching the TV in the corner by the cookbooks.

"Turn that off and go upstairs," Ruth said.

"A dirty, smelly man followed me today."

"Go!" Her mother pointed toward the stairs.

"I ran to get away from him but he found me again. He thought it was funny that I was afraid of him in broad daylight on a busy street. I could smell him and he could smell me."

Ruth's face filled with concern. "He didn't hurt you, did he?"

Joey shook her head. "But you know something. I'm afraid of most men. Not Ray or Charlie, though I was at first. Strange men."

"You need to be. There are crazies out there."

"I know I should be afraid on some level, but not the way I am. There's caution and then there's this . . . this terror." She punched her own stomach. "Today, I felt that terror."

Ruth squeezed her eyes shut. "Did anyone help you?"

"No one noticed at first." Joey looked straight at her mother. "He was so disgusting that I thought he might be Daddy."

Ruth, with her towel-wrapped hand raised, gnawed her bottom lip but said nothing.

Joey walked over and pulled some paper towels from the roll by the sink. "When I was running from him, I thought he was really tall, you know, a big man. But when I stood up and faced him, he was little and kind of shriveled, like somebody real old, except he wasn't." She squatted down and dabbed at her mother's blood. "Some people stopped and he ran away." She looked up. "But I had already won."

"What do you mean?"

"I'd quit running."

A look came to her mother's eyes. Joey had seen the same look in the eyes of the homeless men in San Francisco, sitting like rocks in a stream, their backs to a wall, still breathing but finished with living. "I wish I knew what that felt like," Ruth said.

No lights were on in the living room and the only light on in the kitchen was the one over the stove. Joey and her mother were standing by the sink with their arms around each other when the high beams of Ray's truck came down the driveway, exposing the room as if a flash had gone off.

Ruth wiped her eyes and turned away from the glare. Luke barreled down the stairs and out the front door to meet him. Joey waved before he doused the headlights.

The next morning, Ruth began calling the list of places that might take Sukari. She started with the Wildlife WayStation in California, then Primarily Primates in San Antonio, the place closest to where Sukari was being held.

When her mother hung up, she was changed. She'd made the first two calls as if she expected this to work out with little effort, but there was something about the way she poked the next name on the list and started to dial.

Joey stopped her. "What did they say?"

"That none of the places they know of has any room. Joey"—she gnawed her lip—"there are nineteen hundred chimps in labs and hundreds more in circuses, and movie chimps too old to be cute anymore. They called them 'surplus chimps,' as if they were out-of-date canned goods. There are just too many in need of someplace to go."

"Maybe you were right all along." Joey sank into the plush cushions of the sofa and put her head in her hands.

Ruth came across the room, sat down, and put her arms around Joey. Joey felt her lips moving and her warm breath against her hair. She looked up. "What were you saying?"

"Just that you'll always know you tried your best."

Through the blur of her tears, Joey's gaze focused on the stark white scar that split her mother's left eyebrow into two halves. Was there a moment like this when her mother was a girl, a moment when she chose to give in rather than fight? It would be easier to give up, and the next time it would be easier still. How many times had her mother conceded before it became her habit? How many times can you throw up your hands in defeat, before adopting "I can't" as your song. "Not me," Joey said, shook her mother off, and stood up. "I haven't tried my best. Not yet. And neither have you."

"Well, what do you think we can do with nearly two thousand chimps needing to be rescued?"

"I don't care how many there are. We have only one and we have to find her a place. I'm not giving up after two tries. It's easier if you make the calls, but I'll find someone with a TTY and do it myself if I have to."

Her mother's face filled with pity. "Honey, there's no . . ."

"Start with the man in Washington who has Washoe." Joey took her hand and dragged her from the sofa to the phone.

Ruth shook her head, sadly, but ran her finger down the list to Roger Fouts at Central Washington University. She got his wife, Debbie, who didn't know of any openings but referred her to Shirley McGreal, head of the International Primate Protection League. Shirley recommended the Jane Goodall Institute.

And so it went. Joey kept an eye on Luke while her mother called and called until everyone was recommending places she'd already talked to. She hung up finally and sat massaging her ear.

Joey took the stool across the counter from her.

"There's nothing. Not one place."

"There's got to be."

"I've tried everyone on the list and four more that were recommended by the ones I called. There's no one left. They don't have cages for any more than they've got. They did add her to their wait-lists. Beyond that, I don't know what else to do."

Joey got up and began to pace the kitchen. "Did you tell them how special she is? That she uses sign language?"

" 'Special' means nothing. There is no space. The last place told me to give up, that even if I found a place with room for her, they wouldn't take her because she can't go in with other chimps. None of them could afford an enclosure just for her. And that doesn't address the funding needed to feed the ones they have."

"Funding?"

"They all operate on donations, so none of them have much money."

"Call them all back."

"What?"

"Call 'em back, Mom. Sukari is the only one who comes with money."

"What do you mean?"

"Charlie made me her guardian and set up a trust fund for her. She's got lots of money and I'm the boss of it."

All the years that Ruth continued to wait tables at the Old Dock Café had taught Joey how much her mother believed in the protective power of money. She picked up the receiver and handed it to her mother, then crossed her fingers and held them behind her back as her mother began to dial.

The first three facilities couldn't take her because they had no place to keep her isolated from other chimps for the time it would take to build a new enclosure. Then Ruth called the Center for Great Ape Conservation in Miami, Florida.

Her mother had been sitting with the phone clamped between her ear and shoulder, tired and exasperated-looking. She sat up suddenly and covered the mouthpiece. "We may have something," she said to Joey.

"Oh, I'm so sorry," her mother said into the receiver.

Joey's heart sank.

"Yes, sure, that would be fine." Ruth gave Joey a thumbs-up. "A few weeks?" Her mother's expression was quizzical.

"I don't know how long it will take me to get her out," Joey whispered.

"*You* get her out?" she said, then into the phone: "Sorry, Pam, I was talking to my daughter. We don't know exactly how long it will take," she said, cutting Joey a look. "I'm very sorry for your loss, but we'd nearly given up hope. Yes. Yes. As soon as

I know something. Thank you." She hung up. "One of her orangutans is dying of cancer. Sukari will have his cage all to herself."

"Oh, Mom, that's wonderful." Joey hugged her quickly, then handed her the receiver again. "Call Mr. McCully and tell him, will you?"

"First tell me what you meant about you getting her?"

"I don't know," Joey answered. "It just slipped out; I hadn't thought about it until I said it, but I want to go get her. It has to be me."

"That's impossible."

"So was finding a place for Sukari."

Chapter Fourteen

The call from Pam Rowland that her orangutan had died came the day after Thanksgiving. Joey was in the yard helping her stepfather mulch her mother's sickly-looking flower garden when Ray tapped her shoulder. Her mother stood in the door, her face giving nothing away, yet Joey's heart began to pound. She was as certain that the call had come as if she'd answered the phone herself. She hugged a surprised-looking Ray and ran to her mother. The message was "whenever you're ready."

The argument about how soon lasted all weekend. Joey wanted to go right away. Her mother said that if she insisted on going herself, she had to wait until the Christmas holidays, when Ray could get off work and go with her. She wasn't traveling to New Mexico and Florida by herself. That was final.

"I don't want her to have to stay there another month."

"You told me Mr. McCully got an injunction to stop the testing, so she's not being hurt. Another few weeks one way or the other won't matter."

"It matters to me."

"Look, Joey, it will take some time to make all the travel plans and get tickets. By the time I get that done for you, you'll only have to wait another week or two. You won't miss school, Ray will be off work. . . ."

Joey put her hands behind her back and crossed her fingers. "Okay," she said. She didn't know how she'd do it, but she wasn't going to leave Sukari there a minute longer than she had to, certainly not another month.

At school on Monday, she used the relay operator to call Mr. McCully. He was out, so she left the message with his secretary: "Could he do something to help me move Sukari right away?"

The next morning at breakfast, an aide found her in the cafeteria to tell her she had a call.

"Joey, Mr. McCully here. Everything is set. You'll be met in Albuquerque by an associate of mine and an interpreter. Would you rather fly or take the train? GA."

"A train would be easier. GA."

"And more comfortable. Hang on." No words came across the screen for a moment or two, then they started again: "My secretary says there's a ten P.M. train out of Emeryville. It arrives at noon the next day in Albuquerque. A courier will deliver the tickets and some expense money. They won't let Sukari travel by train, which is just as well. Once you've got her, you'll want to get her to her new home quickly. I'll book a flight to Miami out of either Albuquerque or El Paso, depending on the schedules. Do you want the other tickets in your mother's name? GA."

Joey's heart leapt. Should she say yes so he'd think her mother was going? She hesitated; then, without knowing what she was about to say, she typed in a half-truth: "No, sir. She can't get off work and has no one to leave Luke with. Nobody's going with me." She held her breath then typed, "GA."

"Are you comfortable going alone? GA."

"Yes, sir. I travel alone all the time, nearly every weekend. GA."

"I'd love to be there myself, but I have a trial starting Monday. Call me if you need anything and good luck, my friend. GA."

Joey stood staring at the blank screen wondering, *Now what?* until she realized the secretary was looking at her. ANOTHER CALL? she asked.

NO, THANKS. Joey started for the door, stopped, and turned. CHANGE MIND, PLEASE. NEED CALL MOTHER.

Joey told Ruth that Michelle's mother wanted her to baby-sit over the weekend. If her mother didn't check, which she'd never done, Joey wouldn't be expected home until the weekend after next. It took her another day to think what to tell Michelle and the office that would give her the school week off. She had the answer by morning—donated by one of her nightmares.

She awoke, as she often did, with the sheets knotted in her fists. Her mother's screams rang in her ears as clearly as they had when she could hear. It was Joey's sixth birthday and the cake her mother had baked lay smashed on the floor, beneath a circle of chocolate icing on the wall.

That afternoon, Joey, who could not remember lying more than once or twice in her life, told Michelle, and then the school counselor, that she was going home for a few days to help her mother with her brother's fifth-birthday party. Her mother, she told them, had fallen on the stairs and dislocated her shoulder. With crossed fingers jammed into the pockets of her jacket to ease her guilt, she told an elaborate story of how her mother had tripped on the stairs but stopped her fall by catching the banister. Doctors said the injury to her shoulder had saved her from breaking her neck. Joey guessed the school might send a get-well card, but not until Monday, and it would take a couple of days to get there. Michelle's mother might call, but she'd be too scattered to think about it until Monday when the household settled down after a hectic weekend. By that time Joey would be in Miami with Sukari.

Early Friday morning, she caught a bus to Emeryville. Once on board the train, the attendant came by to check tickets. Joey had only glanced at them herself to make sure that there were train tickets to Albuquerque and plane tickets from El Paso to Miami. She settled into her seat on the train thinking she would read and sleep and wake up tomorrow in Albuquerque. The attendant, as usual, wrote the destination code on a card and fitted it into a slot on the overhead luggage rack. Joey sat in the window seat. She could see the cards of the people across the aisle, but not her own. They were getting off in BFD, wherever that was.

Joey hadn't slept for days, first worrying about whether she'd get caught before she got away and then about the condition she'd find Sukari in. She forced herself to stay awake through the Fresno stop because she wanted to see if it had changed since she'd last seen Sukari.

In Fresno, she stared out the window, comforted by the trees that were taller and bare of leaves. As they pulled out, she wondered why she felt better. What comfort were trees in winter? Just before she drifted off to sleep, she remembered how grateful she'd been that the people who now owned Charlie's house had changed the way it looked. She needed the world to change, even a little. It should not go on without noticing that important people were missing.

A man in overalls carrying a vacuum cleaner shook her. "What are you doing here?"

Joey blinked and sat up, rubbing her eyes. "What?" She looked around. The train was stopped and empty.

An attendant rushed up and snatched the destination card from above her seat and showed it to her. It read "BFD." "The bus left hours ago."

"What bus? I'm going to Albuquerque."

"Yes, but you have to . . ." The attendant pulled Joey's suitcase from the overhead rack, so Joey missed the rest of what she said.

Joey patted her coat pockets, searching for her hearing aids. She hadn't missed them and now realized they were still on her dresser. "I'm deaf."

The woman paled. "You can't hear?"

Joey shook her head.

"Oh, man."

As it turned out, this train ended its run in Bakersfield, California. She was to have gotten off and taken a connecting bus to Los Angeles to catch the Southwest Chief from there to Albuquerque. The station manager and a conductor came running when the attendant radioed them. Both men's lips were thin and compressed, impossible to read, but they were clearly mad at her.

"I have to be on that train," Joey said, trying desperately not to cry. "It's very important."

The station manager said something, then took her by the arm and rushed her off the train, roughly, as if she'd stowed away. They took her into the station and made her sit, as if she were a child, or not too bright. She felt she deserved their anger. If she'd only looked at her tickets, she'd have seen that there was a bus coupon there. Maybe her mother was right not to want her traveling so far alone. If she couldn't be trusted to remember her hearing aids when she was going clear across country by herself, she probably wasn't responsible enough to make the trip. Joey got up and went to the office door. The station manager was talking on the phone. "I'm sorry that I missed the bus," she said, "but you have to get me on that train."

The man waved for her to be quiet. The attendant came toward her, pointing toward the chair she'd just left. "You go sit out there."

Joey took a step backward, then flushed. *The only thing you can't do is hear,* Charlie had written. "I'm deaf, not re-tarded," she snapped. "Don't talk to me like that."

"I . . . I'm sorry," the attendant said, then suddenly realized that Joey had understood her. "You read lips."

"Yours pretty well. Not his."

The attendant looked at the manager, then back at Joey. "We've got a taxi coming to take you to Barstow to meet the Southwest Chief. It left L.A. on time."

Joey's knees wobbled, she was so nervous. She caught "taxi

coming" and "Barstow." She pretended to understand completely. "I don't think I can afford to take a cab to Barstow. How far is it?"

"About a hundred and thirty-six miles."

Joey unzipped her backpack and took out her wallet. Mr. McCully had sent her $250. "I don't think I have enough to pay for the cab, but here is the number of an attorney in San Francisco. I'd like to call him."

"You don't understand. Amtrak will pay for the cab."

"Really?"

The attendant nodded. "If you'd told me you were deaf . . ."

"I know, I should have, but I didn't know about the change and you didn't say anything when you checked my ticket."

The attendant shot the manager a look, then walked Joey from the office. "Do you need to use the restroom or anything? It will be a long ride."

The cab ride through the dark desert night was wild. The driver had been told she was deaf, so he hunkered over the steering wheel, wordlessly, and drove as if they had a fire-breathing dragon on their tail. Joey spent the ride terrified they would crash and terrified they'd miss the train. At one point, he pulled into a gas station to use the pay phone. When he returned, he said, "It's nip and tuck," then shrugged, got in, and sped out of the parking lot, tires squealing.

The train was sitting in the station with only one door open. As the taxi careened to a stop, the attendant waved for her to run. Joey crushed a twenty-dollar bill into the driver's hand, flung open the door, and ran for the train.

The second she leapt aboard, the attendant waved to the

engineer, slammed the door, and the train started to roll. "You waited for me?" she gasped.

He smiled, took a pencil from his pocket, and wrote, *You must be pretty important,* on a little pad.

"I'm not," Joey said, tears streaming down her cheeks, "but I'm meeting someone who is."

Mr. McCully had reserved a deluxe sleeper for her. When the attendant led her through the car and slid open the door to room B, Joey couldn't believe her eyes. There was a sofa, a swivel chair, and her own little bathroom. The decor was a bit tired-looking, but she sank into it gratefully.

She'd missed dinner and the dining car was closed, but a few minutes after she boarded, the attendant brought her a tuna sandwich and a bag of chips. While she ate, he turned the sofa into a bed. Joey's last thoughts, before sleep overwhelmed her, were of Sukari comforting Luke that day in the yard after he ran into the power pole. Joey hadn't understood the signs then but she'd remembered them now. Sukari was hugging Luke and when he stopped crying and grinned, her solemn little face lit up and she signed, HURT GO. HAPPY. As the train rolled through the night, Joey's last thought was that her own happiness depended on believing that someday, no matter what they'd done to her, Sukari's pain, too, would end.

Chapter Fifteen

Though it had been less than a month since Joey learned where Sukari was, she'd had plenty of time to imagine this day. She'd tried to steel herself, but nothing in her worst nightmare could have prepared her for what she was about to see.

Dolores Miller, an attorney friend of Mr. McCully's, and Kathy Lawson, a sign language interpreter, met her at the train station in Albuquerque. From there they drove in a rented van with a large cage in the back for more than five hours to Alamogordo, New Mexico, a small town near White Sands, where the first atomic bomb was tested, and just southeast of Roswell, where the first aliens from outer space supposedly landed.

Joey knew that if aliens had landed anywhere near here, it must have been by mistake. She'd never seen such desolation. The only color out the van window on the drive down Interstate 25 was beige. The mountains, dotted with short, dull green scrubs, were beige. The flatland, pocked with gray-green sage, was beige.

Ms. Miller drove and Kathy rode shotgun. Joey had wanted

to sit in the backseat and not talk, but Kathy tried to include her by interpreting everything that she and Ms. Miller said. How warm they thought it was for early December, how long since it had rained, and so on.

At San Antonio, they took SR 380, a two-lane road that seemed to drift randomly south. There was nothing for miles before they went through the single two-house town of Bingham. Kathy pointed out that the man in the first house sold maps to the Trinity Site, where the first atomic bomb was tested, and the owner of the second house had a rock shop that sold "trinitite," soil from the blast site turned to molten glass by the heat of the explosion.

Joey appreciated that they were all trying not to think about the task that lay ahead, but she finally pretended to sleep for the peace closing her eyes brought. She must have dozed off, because when Kathy patted her knee, she started.

WE HERE, she signed as they slowed to turn right into Holloman Air Force Base. A guard, absurdly dressed in jungle camouflage against such a barren background, put one hand on the large pistol on his right hip and held up his left hand for them to stop. Another guard stepped out of the little gatehouse and stood rigidly, watchfully, his rifle at the ready.

"Is this the right place?" Joey asked.

Kathy only nodded, afraid, Joey guessed, to move her hands.

Ms. Miller showed the guard a copy of the court order for Sukari's release. Joey could see none of the conversation that ensued and Kathy's hands remained knotted in her lap, but after a phone call, they were directed to pull into the small parking lot across from the gatehouse. A few minutes later, another armed guard wheeled into the parking lot on two of his jeep's four wheels. He led them to the main entrance, where they were asked to produce identification and again show the court order.

Kathy jumped when the guard reached in and slapped a temporary pass onto the inside of their windshield. Ms. Miller remained tight-jawed and unflinching, staring straight ahead while they waited for the security police to escort them to the Clarke Foundation.

For most of the six- or seven-mile drive, Joey sat forward and center in the backseat. When they passed the German Air Force Headquarters they looked at each other.

"This place gives me the creeps. We could disappear and no-body'd know what became of us," Kathy said, but signed only the first part for Joey, who guessed the rest by catching "disappear" and "what became --- us."

They passed the USAF Space Command and Surveillance Squadron, a large, dark brown cinderblock building with no windows. It was ringed by a high chain-link fence topped off with coils of razor wire. In spite of herself, Joey grinned. "Do you think this is all here because of the aliens?

Ms. Miller finally smiled. "These probably *are* the aliens."

Kathy laughed and interpreted.

Joey was thinking that this must be the longest seven miles on the planet, when they made a turn onto Vandergrief Road, and there, far off to the right, on the broad flat horizon like a dead snake in the sun, she saw a long, single-story building. She knew this was it, and her heart began to pound.

The approach off Vandergrief brought them to the back of

the building. They drove its length, past a series of metal doors, each with a chain-link enclosure attached.

"Dear God," Kathy said.

Ms. Miller made a right turn past the sign that read, CLARKE FOUNDATION, PRIMATE BIOMEDICAL RESEARCH LABORATORY, and pulled into the parking lot. Two scruffy-looking bushes and a straight-backed chair against the front wall beneath a row of windows were all that broke the monotony of the beige building. Joey opened the sliding van door and got out.

About a half mile away, she could see more than a hundred corn cribs shimmering in the heat like a mirage on the desert landscape. She stared at them. "Ask him what those are," she whispered to Kathy.

"Monkeys," the guard said.

Maybe it was the dry heat, but Joey felt dizzy. Was Sukari out there? Did he say monkeys because he didn't know the difference, or were they really monkeys?

"Not chimpanzees?"

"No, monkeys," he said. "A thousand of them. Come this way. I want to see Dr. Fred's face when he gets this." The security guard grinned and waved the court order.

An old dog with fur the color of sand lifted his head to look at them as they came in the glass doors, then laid it down again and thumped the floor with his tail. They waited in the shabby lobby with the dog until the guard came back.

About midway down the corridor, standing in the only open doorway, was a short, round, wispy-white-haired old man in baggy, wrinkled gray pants held up by suspenders. Joey thought of the empty chair against the building and guessed it belonged to him. She pictured him out there till the sun came up over the roof, content to watch the jets scream across the sky, or the quieter comings and goings of the people who worked here. As they approached, she saw the stub of a cigar clamped in his teeth and his icy stare. After they passed, she glanced back and saw him crush the court order in his fist, go back into his office, and close the black-lettered door: DR. FREDRICK CLARKE. DIRECTOR. The man who owned and ran the most notorious research lab in the country was a dumpy, angry old man. If she wasn't who she was and wasn't steps away from taking Sukari away from him, she might not have believed it was possible for men like him and her father to exist in the world, which otherwise seemed relatively compassionate.

Inside a locker room, they were asked to dress in white jumpsuits made of Tyvek, the same material that the addition to their house had been wrapped in before the siding went on. They pulled on black rubber boots just like the ones she'd been wearing the day she met Charlie and Sukari, and they were fitted with white hoods and plastic faceplates with headbands. They looked like astronauts and she was afraid Sukari wouldn't recognize her. But when she asked why they had to dress this way, the "Animal-Care Technician" who had joined them said that it was for protection from the chimps who spit and threw food and feces at the workers. A knot formed in Joey's stomach. *Have they turned Sukari into that kind of chimp?*

They left the locker room and passed through a set of double doors marked NO ADMITTANCE: LAB PERSONNEL ONLY, into a fluorescently lit, windowless room lined with cages of screaming, howling, wide-eyed monkeys, some in barred cages, others in aquarium-like plastic boxes. Pairs of baby monkeys rushed to hug each other, then huddled, trembling in the far corners of their cages, staring at the procession with shattered eyes. Joey slowed like someone passing a cruel, crushing accident. She didn't want to see, yet couldn't look away. One of the babies, alone in a bare box the size of a bicycle basket, eyed them with fear and longing, then came shyly to the front and followed their progress like a mime, its pink, wrinkled palms moving along the plastic window. Joey stopped and brought a finger to touch the baby's, but the care-tech stepped forward and shook her head.

Ms. Miller grabbed Joey's arm at the same time. She was very pale. "I can't do this," she said, swaying slightly. "I'll . . . I'll be with the dog." She spun and pitched through the swinging doors.

A hurt look came to the care-tech's narrow face. "The work we do here saves lives."

Kathy's face was white and streaked with tears as she interpreted for Joey.

The baby monkey had knotted itself into the corner of its little aquarium. When Joey glanced at it again, it began to tremble. Joey put a hand on Kathy's arm. "Are you okay to go on?"

Kathy nodded.

Though this room had recently been washed down with the black rubber fire hoses that were dripping at each end of the gray concrete room, it still reeked. Joey knew this smell—she'd smelled it on her mother and on herself. The room was saturated with an odor that no amount of Clorox could cover—the stench of fear.

Joey's mother once had a suede coat with a fox collar. She'd kept it stored, saving it, not for special occasions, of which there were none, but for emergencies, like job interviews. She hoped that if she looked as if she didn't really need work, they'd be more inclined to hire her. People with jobs to offer were like banks, she told Joey—the less you looked as if you needed the money, the more likely they were to want to loan you some.

The coat and its collar were probably long gone; she hadn't seen it in years, but she still remembered the vague mothball smell, and running to greet her mother. She remembered being lifted and hugged and burying her face in the soft cloud of fur and feeling it tickle her cheek and neck. She'd been too young to wonder about the animals that had died for the coat and its collar any more than she made the link between live chickens, cows, or pigs and what she ate.

Now, crossing this room, she imagined the fox, whose fur had made that collar, one foot clamped in a steel-jaw trap, frantically trying to gnaw its own leg off. How did they ever rid the fur of that smell of terror?

As they neared the next set of doors, Joey tried to visualize what the room where they had Sukari looked like. She needed to blunt the actual moment by imagining it in stages: cages with bars like in prison, concrete floor with drain holes, windowless cinderblock walls, dripping fire hoses, and the stench. How much worse could it be than what she'd already seen? She'd made it this far, but her breath came in short gasps. Kathy must have felt the same, because she took Joey's hand as the care-tech pushed a door open and held it for them to pass.

Entering this next room would forever remain the one

moment when Joey was grateful to be deaf, though not deaf enough. The cages stood on six-inch legs and were about six feet square. The sides, tops, and bottoms were fat aluminum bars, and they were bare inside except for a narrow metal shelf for the chimp to lie on. There was a large metal box attached to each cage door for food and a stainless steel nipple for water. Each cage held a single chimpanzee. A few charged their bars, gripped them with feet and hands, and screamed and hooted. Others threw food and feces and spit at them through bared teeth. Kathy stepped closer to Joey, then maneuvered her to the center of the aisle as they followed the tech.

A few chimps ran to the bars and held out their hands with pleading looks.

"These are our Special K addicts," the care-tech said, dodging the outstretched hands. Kathy interpreted, and must have asked what that meant, because the tech added, "They're addicted to Ketamine, the tranquilizer we use."

Midway down the row of cages, they came to a lab technician drawing blood from a chimp who was pressed against the back wall by the door of its own cage. As if they were a tour group, their tech stopped. "This is a new kind of cage called a 'squeeze-back,' which means," she explained, "we no longer have to do a knock-down"—she stopped to puzzle how to define this for them—"you know, tranquilize the subjects for routine exams. Though, as you can see, some of the chimps that are tested daily are addicted to the tranquilizer and really miss it." She smiled.

As Kathy's trembling hands repeated this for Joey, the tech was hit in the shoulder with a blob of what looked like soggy brown cereal. She absently spread the slime down her arm with a gloved hand. "They fill their cheeks with water and their Jumbo Biscuits and spit that at us, too." She shrugged.

Joey felt as if she'd lost all sensation; a numbness moved from her head to her feet and she thought she might faint. She bit down as hard as she could stand on her bottom lip, so that she'd have a physical pain to focus on. She moved forward, concentrating on one foot, then the other. When the tech stopped again, Joey stared straight ahead. Kathy touched her arm. She turned and saw that the cages were numbered. They were standing in front of CF1029. Joey blinked to focus. The chimp was crammed into the corner of its cage, beneath its metal sleeping shelf. She could see only its legs. The same number was tattooed on one of its thighs.

The tech had a list attached to a clipboard with a plastic sheet for protection. It reminded Joey of the Etch A Sketch that Smiley had given her all those years ago. The tech wiped it with her arm, then ran a finger down the numbers and across the line. "This is the one."

Joey's knees were weak and offered no resistance as she sank to the floor. The chimp sat in the corner, staring blankly and rocking.

"Sukari?" Joey whispered.

There was no response, and for a moment Joey thought that either it wasn't Sukari or she couldn't be heard through the face shield and over the screams of the other chimps. She was turning to ask the technician if she was sure when she saw the chimp's fingers moving.

Joey reached up slowly and took off the face shield and her hood. "Sukari, it's me. Joey."

Sukari stopped rocking and drew her legs in tight. She glanced at Joey just as the care-tech squatted down to watch.

Sukari screamed and jammed herself deeper into the corner, signing, NO HURT. HUG. HUG.

"Get away," Joey cried, and shoved the tech, who tipped over and landed on her butt.

"We're very good to these animals," she snapped.

Kathy suddenly ripped her hood off. Her face was scarlet and she gasped for air. She turned to the tech. "That chimp signed, 'No hurt. Hug. Hug.'"

"I always wondered what that meant," the tech said.

Kathy managed to interpret this for Joey, then added, SORRY ME, and fled toward the doors past the outstretched hands of the addicted and through a rain of spit, food, and feces.

Between the smell and the grief, Joey thought she was going to throw up. She gagged, then swallowed again and again, trying to get control.

When the tech touched her shoulder, Joey screamed, "Get away from us."

The woman backed away.

Joey sat on the floor.

"Sukari," she whispered, over and over. "It's Joey."

Sukari's frightened eyes shifted from the tech to her. Joey signed, I-SEE-YOU.

Sukari stared at Joey for a full minute, as if she expected her friend's face to wisp away. But in her lap her hands moved, repeating, J-Y HERE? J-Y HERE?

"Yes, honey. I'm here."

HELP ME, PLEASE.

"Oh God," Joey cried. "Get her out of there. Get her out." She grabbed the bars and jerked on them.

"Not safe," the tech said in large, exaggerated words behind her faceplate. "Knock-down first."

"Get her out," Joey shrieked and grabbed the tech's arm.

The woman, with trembling hands, unlocked the door, swung it open, and leapt backward as if she'd freed a monster.

NO HURT, Sukari signed, still pressed to the back of the cage. GOOD GIRL ME. HUG. HUG.

Joey sobbed. NO HURT. COME HUG. She offered Sukari the back of her hand.

Walking across the barred cage floor was hard and Sukari came out unsteadily on all fours. At the opening, she stopped and sat on her haunches. TURTLE HERE? she asked.

"No, honey. Turtle's not here."

Joey lifted her out and struggled to her feet, hugging her thin, weakened friend as tightly as she dared. She started for the door, then stopped and went back to face the care-tech. "Genetically, chimps are over 98 percent human; that's more human than you people are."

Chapter Sixteen

With her arms and legs wrapped tightly around her, Sukari buried her face against Joey's neck as she was carried past the other chimps, through the doors, past the cages of baby monkeys, then down the long corridor to the lobby. Clarke's door was ajar, but Joey could not see if he watched them. In the lobby, Joey covered Sukari's eyes as they rushed past the dog, whose tail thumped the floor.

In the parking lot, dust devils, gritty little tornadoes of sand, swirled around, picking up bits of trash. Joey covered Sukari's eyes again to keep out the blowing sand and ran with her to the van as if, with safety so close, they might be snatched back. Kathy opened the van door and Ms. Miller started the engine. The moment Joey and Sukari were safely inside, Ms. Miller gave it the gas.

Though she was sure she must have taken a breath at some point on the seven-mile drive back, Joey felt as if she had held it until the security guard in the jeep dropped off at the front gate and the military guard waved them through. At that point, she hugged Sukari and laughed out loud. Kathy congratulated her; Ms. Miller gave her a wink in the rearview mirror, then they fell silent, as if ashamed of their joy when they'd left such misfortune behind.

Joey had noticed that a road driven in one direction may look entirely different on the ride back. The road out of Alamogordo was an exception. It looked the same going as it had coming. Nothing redeemed the place.

Ms. Miller, who had driven at an alarming rate from Albuquerque to Alamogordo, drifted just under the speed limit. Kathy stared out the passenger window, lost in thought, with her chin on her fist. Joey sat in the backseat, holding Sukari tenderly, like a soap bubble caught on a fingertip. Sukari snuggled into her lap with an arm around Joey's waist, but her amber eyes stayed glued to Joey's face and her fingers continued to brush her lips, her eyelashes, the tip of her nose, as if Joey were a mirage that in Sukari's mind still threatened to dissolve.

At some point, Joey dozed off with her cheek against the top of Sukari's head, but was startled awake when Sukari plucked her sleeve. MAKE DIRTY ME.

Kathy, who had turned when Joey's foot kicked the back of her seat, interpreted Sukari's rubbery signs for Ms. Miller, though Joey had to translate "make dirty" as "use the toilet" for them both.

They were in Las Cruces, about to get on Interstate 10 headed south to El Paso, where she and Sukari would catch the America West all-night flight to Miami. There were three gas stations vying for business at the on-ramp, but all of them were the new convenience-store types with bathrooms on the inside.

Ms. Miller passed them and drove until she found an old-style station with a bathroom they could pull right up to, out of sight of the office and the pumps. While Joey sneaked Sukari into the ladies' room, Kathy bought them all Cokes and bags of oily, salted peanuts.

Sukari began to relax after that, as if using a real toilet and washing her hands afterward let her trust that being free was not just in her imagination. Once back in the van, she ate her peanuts, drank her Coke, then began to ask questions. WHERE MY BABY? By which Joey guessed she must mean Lynn's daughter, Katie. WHERE HIDEY? WHERE DR. L? WHERE TURTLE? A question that, after nearly two years, continued to worry Joey. Sukari never forgot anyone she loved; could she forgive being deserted by them all?

In response to each question, Joey signed, HOME, the one answer that felt most honest.

GO HOME?

NEW HOME.

J-Y GO?

YES. YOU-ME GO NEW HOME.

Kathy watched in amazement, repeating the conversation for Ms. Miller.

TURTLE NEW HOME?

NO.

WHERE TURTLE?

Joey had packed presents for Sukari and decided to break off the interrogation by shifting her attention. WANT GIFT YOU?

RAISIN?

"Maybe." Joey pretended to hunt through her backpack in vain.

Sukari pushed her face into the search, signing, WANT RAISIN.

Joey handed her a small package, which she'd wrapped and tied up with a bow.

Sukari tore the ribbon with her teeth, then ripped the paper. Inside was a see-through plastic cosmetics bag with a tube of Sukari's favorite-color lipstick, a mirror, a hairbrush, and a comb. She turned it over and over in her hands, touching the items through the plastic.

"They're all yours," Joey said, unzipping it for her.

Sukari routed out the tube of lipstick with a long brown finger. She smeared on the color, then puckered long lips at her image in the mirror.

PRETTY YOU, Kathy signed.

When Joey had visited Sukari in Fresno, she'd found her cage littered with back issues of *Esquire*. Lynn told her that Sukari had begun to show an interest in men, and she loved looking at them in Jack's old *Esquire* magazines. Joey had bought her the latest edition at a stand near the train station in Emeryville along with two small boxes of raisins, the first of which Sukari poured down her throat, but the second box she savored, rolling the raisins between her fingers, enjoying the sticky feel of each and every one.

When she finished the second box, she looked at herself in the mirror again and signed, DIRTY TEETH. She put the mirror down and rubbed the tattoo on her leg. DIRTY. HURT THAT.

"Oh, Lord," Kathy said. Tears filled her eyes and she turned away.

Joey hugged her. "What time does our flight leave?" she asked.

Kathy answered, 11 P.M. NOW 4:30.

"Can we go to a motel? I want to give her a bath."

DIRTY TEETH. DIRTY HURT. Sukari showed her teeth and her leg to them.

They chose a rather shabby-looking motel on the outskirts of El Paso and parked so that the desk clerk couldn't see inside the van. Kathy went in to rent a room, requesting and getting one that didn't face the highway and was, therefore, out of view of the office. After the door was opened and the coast judged clear of maids and passing cars, she signaled to Joey, who ran in with Sukari wrapped in a blanket.

Kathy sat on the toilet lid and Ms. Miller stood in the doorway watching while Joey bathed Sukari with baby shampoo from head to toe. After Joey dried her, Sukari turned the water on and climbed back into the tub, pointed to the tattoo, and signed, MORE BATH.

Joey couldn't stand watching Sukari try to scrub the number off her leg. She carried the room's desk chair over to the vanity for her to stand on to brush her teeth. She unpacked the Mendocino T-shirt and an old pair of Luke's shorts she'd brought for Sukari and laid them out on the bed. After she'd fished her out of the bath and dried her again, Joey tried to dress her, but Sukari broke away and ran back to the tub.

Joey bit her lip. "It's a boo-boo, honey. You can't wash it off."

MORE BATH, PLEASE.

BATH, TV, WHICH?

Sukari ran to the bed, crawled up, and sat on the edge. When Joey found a *Cheers* rerun, Sukari let herself be dressed while she pant-hooted at Sam.

Joey had nipped one of Ray's Mendo Mill baseball caps and Luke's old Mickey Mouse backpack. She put the hairbrush, lipstick, and mirror inside, helped Sukari strap on the pack, then lifted her so she could see herself fully clothed and wearing her cap in the mirror over the sink. For a moment Sukari stared at her image, then lightly touched the reflected face. Joey felt tears threaten until Sukari pointed to herself in the mirror and signed, DEVIL THERE WANT RAISIN.

Since there was nothing her mother could do to stop her now, Joey asked Kathy to call home for her.

Ruth's initial reaction was pretty obvious. Kathy identified herself, but after she explained from where she was calling and for whom, she had to hold the receiver away from her ear. MAD, she signed.

"Please tell her I'm fine and that I'll call her from Miami."

Kathy repeated it when she got the chance, then held the phone at arm's length. Ms. Miller, who was sitting across the room, made a you're-in-big-trouble face. Sukari covered her eyes.

Joey took the phone. "It's me, Mom, so stop shouting and listen. I'm sorry but I couldn't let Sukari stay there another six weeks or another six days, and if you had seen it, you couldn't be mad. It was awful, Mom. She's tattooed, skin and bones, and she was terrified. I'm sorry that you're upset, but it's done now and I'm taking her to Miami. Mr. McCully arranged everything. Pam is meeting me. Kathy and Ms. Miller are here. I'm safe, and, Mom, so is Sukari. Send Hidey, will you? That's the one thing Sukari wants back that we can give her. Love to Luke and Ray." She handed the phone back to Kathy and grinned. "I'm so glad I'm deaf."

Kathy smiled and took the receiver. She nodded a few times, then hung up.

MOTHER OKAY NOW. KNOW-WHAT? IN HEART, PROUD YOU, THINK ME.

As they were preparing to leave the motel, Joey realized that she didn't have anything with which to drug Sukari. The thought of her awake during the flight, alone in a cage in the cold, dark baggage compartment, was unbearable. As soon as she mentioned it, Kathy began searching the local phone book. It was nearly eight when she finally found a vet who was willing to return to his office.

The surly-looking vet took one look at Sukari and eyed them suspiciously. It took Ms. Miller showing him a copy of the court order and Sukari's tattoo to prove she'd been held at Clarke's before he agreed to give them the sedative instead of calling the police.

His instructions were to give her as many pills as possible an hour before departure. Joey had planned on waiting for the flight in the van so Sukari wouldn't have to be put in the cage before she went to sleep. When Ms. Miller came back from checking them in, she said that the agent had told her they could wait in a small lounge next to an employee bathroom. This meant that she and Kathy could turn the rental van in and catch an earlier flight back to Albuquerque.

Joey was nervous about being left alone, but she didn't tell them. Instead, she encouraged them to go, which they finally agreed to do, but not before they walked them to the lounge to see them settled.

Though she'd been nice, Ms. Miller had maintained her reserve, and Joey, who had been immediately comfortable calling Kathy by her first name, continued to address her formally. Joey, who was as shy about goodbyes as she was about meeting strangers, wondered how to tell her how grateful she was that she'd been there, but before she opened her mouth to thank her, Ms. Miller apologized for leaving her and Kathy at the lab. "I have no excuse," she said as Kathy interpreted. "I just can't bear to see that kind of suffering. Never could." Tears filled her eyes and rolled down her cheeks. "And I'm not sure how I am going to forget it." She knelt suddenly in front of Sukari. "I'm just so glad you're safe."

Sukari didn't move for a moment, then she signed, GOOD GIRL YOU. COME HUG. She held her arms up, and when Joey interpreted what she'd said, the attorney sank to the floor. Sukari put her arms around her, but when she patted her back, Ms. Miller began to sob.

After a few moments, she got control of herself and Joey helped her to stand. She straightened her suit, ran her fingers through her hair, then looked Joey in the eye. "I promise you that I will do everything in my power to close that place down." She hugged Joey quickly, then hurried from the room.

Before she left, Kathy kept Sukari occupied while Joey packed the tranquilizers into individual raisins and mixed them in with the rest of the box. When Joey finished, Kathy kissed the top of Sukari's head. GOODBYE, MY FRIEND.

WHERE GO YOU?

HOME.

SEE TURTLE?

Kathy shook her head. GO MY HOME, she answered, then turned to Joey. YOU OKAY ALONE?

Joey nodded, afraid that if she opened her mouth, she'd beg her to stay.

BEST JOB MY LIFE THIS. Kathy hugged Joey, then grinned. HOPE NEVER DO AGAIN. At the door, she turned. NOT POSSIBLE ME, DO WHAT YOU DID. VERY STRONG YOU. NEED STAY STRONG.

An hour before departure, Joey gave Sukari the box of drugged raisins. Sukari ate slowly as she thumbed through her *Esquire,* kissing the male models she liked best and signing, PRETTY MAN, to herself.

Joey was relieved that it was going so smoothly until she saw Sukari take something from her mouth and drop it between the seat cushions.

WHAT THAT?

SEED.

The box was nearly empty when Joey lifted the cushion. Beneath it were all but one pill, two pennies, and a quarter.

Joey felt a moment of panic, then she remembered the small dining room she'd seen down the hall from the lounge. She took the pills and stood up.

Sukari put her magazine down, slid off the sofa, and took Joey's hand. "You stay right here. If you're good, I'll bring you a Pepsi. Okay?"

GOOD GIRL ME. She climbed back up on the sofa.

The room had two tables, assorted chairs of different styles, vending machines, a microwave, and a miniature refrigerator. There were no cups, so Joey bought coffee from a vending machine, took the cup when it dropped, and let the coffee run down the overflow drain. She got a little water from a fountain by the door, then heated it in the microwave. The pills streamed bubbles and dissolved quickly when she dropped them into the hot water. Joey drank the Pepsi down a little, then poured the pill-mix into the can. She stirred it with the coffee stir-stick and went back to the lounge.

Sukari food-grunted. GOOD GIRL ME. GIVE DRINK.

Ten minutes after she finished the cola, the agent came to tell Joey the flight was boarding.

"She's still awake," Joey said.

Sukari pointed to a picture of a man in her magazine and smiled at the agent.

The woman handed her a note: ***The cage is on a baggage cart and we have someone to drive you to the plane.***

Sukari yawned.

The woman gave Joey a leash, which was a joke. Sukari had the strength of a grown man. Joey dutifully attached the hook to the neck hole of Sukari's T-shirt, but when the agent turned to go, Joey gave Sukari the loop to hold.

GO WALK, Sukari signed like a drunk, then stumbled and wobbled erratically in the agent's wake. When she let the leash loop slip from her fingers and had to walk on all fours to keep her balance, Joey picked her up. "Are you a sleepy girl?"

NO, she answered, but her eyes drooped and she put her head on Joey's shoulder.

By the time the car got to the airplane, Sukari was snoring softly. Before Joey put her in the large cage, she diapered her, covered the floor with a blanket, put a small airline pillow under her head, and put her backpack and magazine in with her. She also fitted her in her own sweater so that she could sleep wrapped in Joey's smell. She stayed and watched Sukari's cage ride the conveyor belt up into the belly before boarding the plane herself.

The ticket agent had told Ms. Miller that one of the flight attendants on board knew a little ASL, but Joey had forgotten. When she boarded, the woman who seemed to be in charge asked her to wait in the galley for a few minutes; Joey missed why.

It turned out that the flight attendant who signed was working the front cabin. When the agent closed the door, there were seats vacant in first-class and Joey was given one in the last row. Joey had never flown and would have been thrilled if she hadn't been so concerned about Sukari. From her window she could see the baggage handlers pitching last-minute bags onto the conveyor belt. She wondered if Sukari was still asleep or they had awakened and frightened her. It wasn't until they pulled the conveyor away and closed the cargo door that Joey began to relax.

As they taxied away from the gate, a pretty blonde in a navy-blue uniform touched her shoulder. DEAF YOU?

"Yes."

MY NAME J-O-A-N-N-E. NAME YOU?

SAME.

COOL.

SIGN NAME J-Y.

The plane made one stop in New Orleans. During the lay-over, Joanne took Joey down to check on Sukari. She had moved only slightly, pulling an arm up so that her nose rested against the wool sleeve of Joey's sweater.

Chapter Seventeen

Joey slept an exhausted, dead-to-the-world sleep after New Orleans and awoke only when the plane thudded onto the runway. Joanne had lowered the shade on her window and covered her with a blanket. Joey lifted the shade to find a blindingly bright morning in Miami.

Pam Rowland was waiting for her in baggage claim. She held a pad in the air with SUKARI & JOEY printed on it in bold, black letters. When Joey waved, she grinned and pushed through the crowd to shake her hand. On the back of the pad she'd written, *I'm so happy you're here.*

Reading the scrawled welcome, Joey felt as if she'd stepped, alive and unhurt, out of the rubble of some disaster. She *was* here. She'd done it; she'd saved Sukari. "I am here, aren't I?" Tears stung her eyes. She started to tremble and barely got out the words, "Thank you for taking us," before she began to sob.

Pam put an arm around her waist and led her out of the crush of people at the carousel where the first bags were arriving.

They leaned against the railing around the baggage-claim area until Joey regained control.

"I'm sorry," Joey said, wiping her eyes on her sleeve. "I'm just tired, I guess."

Pam hugged her suddenly and Joey hugged her back. Though strangers, they shared a love of something so deep that they already knew each other's hearts.

Pam was tiny compared to Joey. When she let her go and stood on tiptoe to scan the crowd around the carousel, Joey looked, too. Doors from the outside swung open and the crowd parted. Joey saw Sukari sitting up with her baseball cap on backward, the way Luke always wore it. She was rubbing her eyes and yawning, but when she saw Joey, she signed, I-SEE-YOU, then hugged her backpack to her chest and waited for the cage door to open.

People crowded around when the cart stopped. They pointed and laughed—dozens of contorted faces with all their teeth showing. Joey, with Pam right behind her, shoved her way through to the cage. "Get back. Get away from her," Joey snapped and opened the door. The crowd backed away as Sukari, dragging all her belongings, climbed wide-eyed into Joey's arms.

Apparently, Joey's deafness was considered a handicap by the parking police, because Pam had been permitted to park her van right outside the door. In seconds, Joey and Sukari were inside and rolling out of the dark, underground baggage-claim area and into the bright, white Florida sun.

They drove the perimeter of the airport, then turned south on Red Road, through traffic like nothing Joey had ever seen.

It took almost as long to drive the ten or so miles from the airport to Sukari's new home in South Miami as it had to drive from Las Cruces to El Paso the day before.

Pam had the van's air conditioner turned on high but the interior stayed hot long enough for sweat to form and drip down Joey's back and from beneath her breasts and armpits. She'd never felt heat like this, and it was as damp as a bathroom after a scalding shower. She stared out the window and strained to find something to love about the place as they crawled along in the glinting steel stream of traffic.

Joey's dread lifted a bit when they reached South Miami. There were more trees. A mile or so farther south and Pam began to grin like a person who knows the candles on the cake are being lit in the kitchen and the singing is about to start.

Joey leaned forward against the restriction of the seat belt as they approached a forest of exotic trees penned in by a high wall of coral. She knew this was it, but her jaw still dropped at the sight of what had to be a twelve-foot-tall Blue and Gold macaw from whose beak the MACAW WORLD sign hung.

They pulled into the banyon-tree-shaded parking lot and drove to a rear entrance. Perhaps sensing Joey's anticipation, Sukari reached up and looped a long arm around Joey's neck and smiled at her.

Pam stopped outside a vine-covered gate and turned off the engine. HOME YOU, she signed to Sukari, then grinned at Joey. "See, an old dog can learn new tricks."

Sukari grinned with fear. DOG BITE.

NO DOG HERE, Joey answered, then explained Sukari's phobia to Pam.

"I'll never use that cliché again."

Joey stepped from the van into the sweltering heat with Sukari balanced on one hip. Pam led them down the path, past a small office. "There's"—she turned, pointed, then turned back—"there you can sleep on."

"I missed that," Joey said.

Pam flinched. "Oh, Joey, I'm so sorry. How thoughtless of me. Is it rude for me to expect you to read my lips?"

"Don't feel bad. Having to always face me is a hard thing for people to remember. And your lips are pretty easy to read. I'll ask you to repeat things I miss."

"Oh, good. Maybe you and Sukari will teach me to sign"—she laughed—"in our spare time. What I said before was there's a sofa-bed in there you can sleep on. I'm so tired most nights I sleep here as often as I sleep at home. Did you get that?"

Joey nodded. She'd gotten enough of it.

They went through another gate in a tall, chain-link fence and past a cage with two young orangutans. One of them came over and put a long, orange finger through the wire.

"This is Chris," Pam said. "He's a love."

A sense of hopefulness rose in Joey like it had at the movie *E.T.,* the last movie she'd seen and heard. She remembered the glow at the tip of E.T.'s finger and how it had lit up the screen and spread out into the theater. Chris's eyes held Joey's as she shifted Sukari to the other hip and put her fingertip to the tip of Chris's. He curled his finger and she slid hers to hook with his. "Friend," she whispered.

FRIEND, Sukari signed, hooking her own index fingers first one way, then the other.

Joey hugged her. "A new friend and a new home." And her optimism grew when Sukari signed, GOODBYE, RED BOY, instead of calling him a bug like she had the chimps when she lived at the zoo.

But Joey's heart sank when she saw Sukari's new home—an old, rusting, cylindrical steel cage, ten feet high and about six feet in diameter. The sleeping platform was new and a tire hung from a single long rope. A colorful beach ball, which looked as if it had expanded in the heat to the point of exploding, lay on the dirt floor.

Pam must have known Joey would be disappointed because she had a note all written: *Don't get bummed. It's only temporary. If she gets along with Noelle and Kenya—and I'm sure she will, in spite of what happened at the zoo—she can move in with them soon.*

"Oh, I hope so," Joey said too quickly, then turned and grabbed Pam's wrist. "I'm sorry. I didn't mean that the way it sounded. I'm so grateful to be here. It's just that she grew up with a room of her own and now, no matter how much I hate it, she has to live in a cage. If I just think about her in that lab, this becomes a castle. It will be fine. I'll stay in it with her for a few days."

Pam laughed and wrote, *I wish I could tell you how many nights I've spent in these cages. You can borrow my lawn chair.*

Macaw World had more different kinds of parrots than Joey imagined there were in the world. Cages full of vividly colored birds lined the walkway to the main entrance. After the place closed that first afternoon, Joey took Sukari to explore her new home. A couple of dozen flamingos, in a pond beyond a patio with concrete picnic tables and a snack bar, seemed to do their dining upside down, but Sukari stared at two white swans for a full minute before deciding, Joey guessed, that neither of them was Gilbert.

Just inside the entrance, an employee was putting away the last of the birds people held to have their pictures taken with. A Blue and Gold macaw held a foot out to Joey, who hesitated only a moment before lifting her arm to let it step on.

Sukari leaned away from its massive beak. BIRD BITE J-Y?

"It doesn't want to bite me." Joey knelt and picked up a sunflower seed. "Give him this."

When the bird stretched its neck to take the seed, Sukari chickened out and threw it down.

Joey picked it up and handed it to the bird, who rolled the small seed in its huge bill, extracted the meat, and let the empty shell float to the ground.

AGAIN, Sukari signed.

Joey picked up another seed and handed it to her. This time Sukari gave it to the macaw, who ate it, then leaned over and caught one of Sukari's big ears by its soft, vulnerable edge. Sukari's lips pulled back in a grimace of fear and she froze, her legs tightening around Joey's waist. But the bird began to preen her gently, running its bill through her thin black hair, across the top of her head and down the back of her neck.

Joey glanced at the man collecting the macaws and smiled, more to herself than at him. What a picture she made in her own mind, a chimpanzee balanced on a hip, a tremendous bird on her arm, two species—three, counting herself—from three different continents. She imagined her mother with a camera, maneuvering to get the background right. Her gaze drifted to the hibiscus hedge and the beautiful birds. She was suddenly astonished that she and Sukari were together again, and in this place.

That first night Joey did borrow Pam's lawn chair and a sleeping bag, and set herself up in the cage with Sukari. Joey tried to get her to use her new platform but they ended up squeezed into the lawn chair together. Only Sukari slept. Joey perspired and watched the giant cockroaches scuttle about on the floor, sides, and ceiling of the cage.

The second night, she waited until Sukari was asleep to try to slip away. Sukari had her by the hand before the door was open wide enough to let another roach in. Pam laughed the next morning, took a can of WD-40, and sprayed the cage-door hinges. "Maybe you'll make it out tonight."

Late the next afternoon, Hidey arrived. Joey and Sukari had gone for a walk and when they returned, his carrier was in her cage. Sukari stopped dead in her tracks when she saw it and began to sway from side to side.

Hidey must have meowed, because Sukari's head jerked, then she looked at Joey wide-eyed. HIDEY THERE?

Joey shrugged, but couldn't cover her smile.

Sukari leaned as close as she could get to the carrier without letting go of Joey's hand. She put an eye to one of the slots, then began to hoot. HIDEY THERE. OPEN. HURRY. HURRY.

When Joey undid the latch, Hidey flopped over on his side, like old times, and let Sukari pull him from the carrier. He hung limply, just as he'd done as a kitten, draped over Sukari's arm, permitting kisses until his back was wet. That night Sukari took Hidey up onto the platform. The hinges had been silenced. When Sukari was asleep, Joey crept from the cage and slept for the first time in days in the air-conditioned, cockroach-free office.

When it wasn't raining or threatening to rain, Pam took the chimps and orangutans for a walk in the afternoon after Macaw World closed and before their evening meal. At her suggestion, Joey and Sukari joined in as a way of testing Sukari's tolerance of the other chimps.

Noelle was two and a half, but Kenya was past four and had lost the white hair tufts on her bottom that mark a baby chimpanzee. They decided to start with just Sukari and Noelle, and of course Chris, the orangutan, whom Sukari seemed to like and who would have been crushed if left behind.

Joey started out carrying Sukari but Noelle, who was familiar with these afternoon playtimes, walked. After only a few yards, Sukari wanted to walk, too. Pam carried Chris, whose feet fit tree limbs beautifully but were not well suited for the ground.

Their destination was a huge old ficus tree, alone in a weedy field at the back of the property. Joey had never seen a tree quite like this. It reminded her of a giant troll. Thin, long roots like coarse hair stretched to meet the ground. Those that had sunk their tips into the sand had thickened so it looked as if the branches had grown legs and were pulling the tree apart in all directions. Sunlight couldn't pierce the canopy, so nothing grew beneath it.

Sukari liked "red boy" and tried to keep his attention on her by signing to him. Noelle, whom she called "black bug," as Joey had feared she would, was tolerated but only if Joey paid no attention to her. If Noelle approached Joey, Sukari charged, screaming and flailing her arms.

On their third trip to the ficus, Sukari climbed high into the tree with Chris, trying to keep up with him as he swung on long arms through the branches. Noelle came down and sat on Pam's lap. When Joey smiled at her, Noelle glanced up to locate Sukari, then came over with her wrist bent. Just as Joey reached to take her hand, Sukari swooped down, grabbed Noelle by the arm, and began to climb with her.

"No," Joey screamed. She jumped up and ran to position herself to catch Noelle if Sukari dropped her. "Bring her down here," Joey demanded.

The tone of Joey's voice must have startled Sukari. She stopped climbing but still dangled Noelle by one arm.

HUG BABY BUG, Joey signed.

Sukari reeled her in and grabbed Noelle around the waist but made no move to let her go or bring her down.

NO HURT BUG, YOU.

J-Y MAD?

YES, J-Y MAD.

J-Y BITE?

"Not if you bring her DOWN right NOW."

Sukari appeared to think about this.

Joey was still wearing the white Macaw World smock that identified her as someone permitted behind the scenes. On their first walk, she'd put an emergency box of raisins in a pocket for just such an occasion as this. J-Y VERY MAD, she signed. WANT BABY BUG. YOU WANT RAISIN?

Sukari started down with Noelle slung over her arm. She stopped on a limb above Joey's head, still out of reach.

"Let her go," Joey said, repeatedly tossing and catching the box of raisins.

Sukari held Noelle out until she grabbed a handful of roots and swung away. J-Y HURT SUKARI?

Joey's heart leapt. She couldn't bear it, if Sukari was afraid of her for even a moment. NO HURT SUKARI. SUKARI NO HURT BABY BUG.

J-Y NEED HUG?

YES.

Sukari swung down until her foot rested on Joey's shoulder, then she let go and fell into her arms.

I-LOVE-YOU, Joey signed. WANT YOU LOVE BABY BUG.

BUG NEED HUG?

YES.

Sukari pulled her lips back as if in disgust but dropped to the ground, then swayed as she lumbered toward Noelle, who grinned with fear.

Joey prepared to charge in, but Sukari sat down suddenly and signed, COME HUG BABY, and held her arms open.

Noelle looked over her shoulder at Pam, who glanced at Joey, then gave Noelle a little shove in Sukari's direction. "It's okay."

Sukari reached out and grabbed Noelle's hand.

Noelle screamed.

Pam started to jump in, but Joey stopped her. Sukari signed, BABY, then forced Noelle's arms into the same shape, one resting on the other, as if cradling a baby, then rocked from side to side. Sukari pointed at her. YOU BABY.

Noelle let her arms drop.

Sukari shaped them again, then poked Noelle's chest. YOU BABY.

Noelle poked Sukari's chest.

NO BABY ME. YOU BABY, Sukari signed.

Noelle flicked leaves with her toes, which made Sukari scream and flail her hands in frustration. She stopped suddenly, then got a sneaky look on her face. TICKLE, she signed, then tickled Noelle, who laughed and rolled on her side.

TICKLE became Noelle's first sign.

By the second week, Kenya and Sukari tolerated each other; Noelle and Sukari were fast friends. Pam decided she was willing to try Sukari in the large cage. Joey said she was glad, but each day she put the move off and each day her mother called to insist she come home. Joey knew that if they successfully moved Sukari in with Noelle and Kenya, she'd be out of excuses to stay. By the end of the week, her desire for what was best for Sukari finally won over her dread of leaving her. On Friday, when they returned from their walk to the ficus tree, they put Sukari in with Noelle and Kenya, then pulled up chairs for the evening vigil. Just before dark, Sukari and Kenya argued over possession of the identical platforms. Kenya won the one she wanted, but Noelle chose to sleep with Sukari and

Hidey. Later that night, Pam booked Joey on Saturday's all-night flight to Oakland.

There was a pond off the trail to the eastern snack bar and Joey liked to go there to "listen" to the water. Late Saturday afternoon, she took Sukari to the pond. With no idea how to explain that she was going home, Joey led her to a concrete bench beside the water and lifted Sukari onto her lap.

"Do you like your new home?" Joey said into her ear.

Sukari put her head back against Joey's shoulder and looked up at her.

Joey signed, LOVE THIS HOME, YOU? Then spread her arms to take in the forest in which they sat.

YES, Sukari answered. J-Y LOVE HOME?

Joey's heart sank. NOT MY HOME.

Sukari lost interest and returned to watching the koi in the pond.

She shifted Sukari off her lap and put her on the bench so they were facing each other. "Sukari, listen to me." J-Y GO HOME, SEE LUKE. Joey made circles in front of her face with the "L" hand, the modified sign for trouble, which she and Sukari had created as a sign-name for Luke.

Sukari scooted off the bench and held out her hand.

NO, YOUR HOME HERE, Joey signed. YOU STAY HERE.

WANT SEE LUKE. GO J-Y HOUSE.

NO, YOU STAY WITH HIDEY.

HIDEY WANT SEE LUKE. HIDEY GO J-Y HOUSE.

NO, YOU STAY WITH BABY BUG.

BABY BUG WANT SEE LUKE.

Joey caught her hands. "You have to wait here for me."

GO J-Y HOUSE, SEE TURTLE.

Joey shook her head. Sometimes she was grateful that Sukari didn't understand death and at other times she wished she did. Joey had disappeared from her life and come back; how hard was it for her to believe that Charlie might come back, too? At least it made Joey hopeful that when she disappeared this time, Sukari would trust her to return. But what concept of time did Sukari have? Joey couldn't tell her she'd be back in June when school was over. Here in Miami, she couldn't even use the changes in the weather to explain that she'd be back when it was hot again. There were no discernible seasons: a little less hot, a little drier, that was it.

In the end, Joey just left. She stayed with Sukari until she was asleep, then Pam drove her to the airport. The air conditioner in the van was broken. Between her grief and the heat, Joey was wringing wet by the time she got there, as if she wept from every pore.

She waited until Tuesday to call Pam from school. At first, Pam tried to sound upbeat, but Joey begged for the truth, then broke down and cried when she got it. Sukari had spent all day Sunday watching the walkway from the office. On Monday, she stayed near the front of the cage, rocking, with Hidey in her lap. When anyone came to the fence that separated visitors from the cage itself, she'd look up expectantly, then resume rocking and signing to herself, WHERE J-Y? WHERE J-Y?

A week later the report was better. After eating nothing but raisins and Cokes, which resulted in terrible diarrhea, she'd finally asked to go on the afternoon walk. After that she acted normal. She resumed eating, and playing with and grooming Noelle. With that news, Joey's heart rested, but every day, when she was least prepared, some small scene from their past played out in her mind, like a special-delivery smile wrapped around a stone of longing.

Epilogue

Four years later
August 29, 1997

Sukari died of liver cancer from the pesticide testing on August 29th. She was ten years old, less than a fifth of her way through her life span. During her last weeks, Joey, who'd taken time off from her biology studies at Gallaudet and preparations for applying to veterinary schools, moved her and Hidey into a small trailer that they'd rented and placed near the ficus tree. The trailer reminded her of life with her father, and she thought her own bad memories would meet her there but instead she felt cocooned. She read to Sukari and they talked about Turtle. Joey told her he'd been waiting and waiting for her and promised that she would see him soon.

WHERE TURTLE?

HIDING.

Sukari smiled.

On the last day of her life, she lay in bed and began to sign for things she wanted brought to her. It started with her stuffed turquoise Miami Dolphin, then her most recent issue of *Esquire*, then the doll Pam had given her—a Raggedy Ann with curly orange hair dyed auburn to match Joey's. She shivered, so Joey covered her with a blanket. She slept then with Hidey beside her, his face buried against her neck.

Joey sat across the room watching Sukari's thin chest rise and fall. "It's time, Charlie," she whispered up at the water-stained ceiling. "Come take your little girl."

Later, when Hidey stood, stretched, and yawned, Joey got up to check on her. She was gone.

A few days later, they all flew back to California, Hidey in his carry-cage strapped into the seat next to Joey and Sukari's ashes in a small oak box in Joey's lap.

She sat by the window and stared out at the slow-moving landscape below. She had seen so much of it from buses, trains, and cars, where it looked either junky and littered, settled with neighborhoods, or wild and pristine. From the plane, she couldn't see the trash, the community, or the beauty. Just squares of carved-up land, cities looking like bits of blown confetti, and highways, apparently empty, except for the occasional flash of light as if someone was signaling with a hand mirror to the sun.

Is this what God sees? she wondered. *And if so, how will things ever change if what can be seen is either too much or too little?*

She'd worn her new, small hearing aids to hear when her flight was called in the terminal and had numbly left them in, not sufficiently bothered by the discomfort of sound to seal herself back into a womb of silence. Throughout the flight, she was vaguely aware of the pilot's announcements of points of interest as they flew over. Though, even with her hearing aids, she could catch only a word or two, she'd glance out anyway.

"Below ---------- left ----------," the pilot said.

When she looked down, a chill swept over her, raising the hairs on her arms. Below them was the deceptively pure pallor of White Sands, New Mexico.

"---------- Home ---------- first ---------- bomb."

The home of large- and small-scale destruction. Joey snatched her hearing aids out and jammed them into her pocket.

Roses were Sukari's favorite flower, to smell and to eat, and red was her favorite color. Joey went to Heartwood Nursery and bought a red-rose bush. She planted it in the sunniest, warmest spot in the yard, and around the base she blended in half of Sukari's ashes.

Her mother, Luke, and Ray came out for the planting. Ray had constructed a wire basket to surround the bush to keep the deer from eating the flowers, but Joey took it off. It looked too much like a cage. Besides, deer fascinated Sukari and the roses would lure them right to her.

A misty rain was falling the day Joey took the rest of her ashes down the back trail to the very largest, oldest, tallest redwood on their property. There was a bench nearby, built when the property was an old-folks home by someone who must have loved this ancient tree as much as she did. She sat there for a long time with the little box of ashes on her lap, watching the creek and remembering moments with Charlie and Sukari, sorting through them like snapshots.

After a while, when the rain became sincere, Joey got up and emptied the box at the base of the tree, then went back to sit on the bench. She watched as the ashes were washed from the surface and deeper into the duff. When they were gone, she lay back, looked up its two-hundred-foot height, and imagined Sukari being gathered by its roots. She watched her scamper to join the flow of water up the xylem, intent on going as high as she could go. Twice, from branches held out like arms, she turned and smiled down at Joey. I-SEE-YOU, J-Y.

"I see you, too, sugar-butt," Joey whispered, then closed her eyes to watch the moment when Sukari's spirit, in a molecule of oxygen, floated free at last.

Afterword

Hurt Go Happy is dedicated to John Hopkins, Lucy, and a dead dog, three individuals who changed my life, and to Belinda, who just needs to be remembered.

At first, when I began to consider the genesis of this book, I didn't go farther back than the 1988 *Houston Chronicle* story about Lucy, a sign-language-using chimpanzee. But the longer I thought about it, the clearer it became that it really started, emotionally, at least, in the summer of 1959, when I was fifteen. I had a fifty-cent-an-hour job working at the Winter Park Day Nursery. Belinda was three years old and a victim of abuse in a time when no one reported things like that. What parents did to their children was their business. From the moment her massively large mother delivered her every morning until she picked her up in the afternoon, Belinda clung to me. I never saw her play with the other children. I certainly never saw her laugh. She was tiny even for three and her bottom and the backs of her little legs were routinely marked with yellowing bruises and the fresh red welts made by the belt her mother used to beat her. So painful were they that I would cradle her when she had to use to the bathroom, so her little bottom didn't press against the toilet seat. I can't bear to think about what became of that child, or that I grew up in a time when dirty looks and the hatred I still carry for that woman was all the power I had. I have often wondered if three short months of kindness made it worse for Belinda. My nightmares are still of what the rest of her life must have been like and of what she became.

The rest of the story starts in 1981. I was a Pan Am flight attendant, flying to London on weekends and going to school during the week, working on an undergraduate degree in biology at the University of Miami. While away one weekend, one of my best friends, Joanne Mansell, found a dog that had sought shelter in the doorway of the Catholic church in Coconut Grove. The dog had been abandoned and was starving. While I was gone, Joanne fed it, trying to gain its trust. Her plan was to drug the dog sufficiently to pick it up and take it to a vet. After I returned, we scraped together all the drugs we could find between us, mostly Dramamine for air-sickness and a Valium or two, and blended them into her can of dog food.

I have never gotten the image of that dog out of my mind as she struggled to her feet and came down the sidewalk toward us, tail wagging. She was young, skin and bones, with no fur left on her body save for a single long patch down the back of her neck. Maggots lived in the open sores on her sides, her eyes were diseased and opaque, and her head and ears were bloody from her miserable digging at the fleas and the flies.

We did the kindest thing for that dog. We took her to the vet and had her put to sleep, but the horror of her existence and how long it might have been since her people abandoned her ate me up. For a week or more, it kept me awake nights until finally, on a layover in London, I got up and wrote her owners an angry letter describing her end. Of course, I had no one to send it to, so it stayed folded in a pocket in my purse for over a year.

Let me say, to that point in my life I'd never written a single creative word. Not one. Being a writer was not a dream of mine; in fact it had never so much as crossed my mind. English was my worst subject in high school. I was good at math and science and had gone back to school with the intention of eventually becoming a vet.

In early August 1982, *The Miami News,* a now-defunct newspaper, was looking for pictures of the Everglade kite, an endangered South Florida hawk. I had some and took them to their offices. Only a couple of days earlier, I had been cleaning out that old purse and found the letter I had written. At the paper, I told the person who was reviewing my slides that if they could use the story, it might make people realize that animals treated like litter for someone else to pick up aren't always taken in. I scrawled *We Found Your Dog* at the top of the page and handed it over.

On August 11th, John Hopkins, an editor with the *News,* called me at home. I was out, but my husband wrote the message down—a single sentence that would eventually change my life: "Tell her," John said, "if she can write like that, we'll publish anything she writes." I was pleased, of course, but my response was that I wasn't a writer. Thanks for calling.

While going through the UM catalog of classes for the fall semester, I saw a creative-writing class listed. On a whim, but with John's call in mind, I enrolled and learned in short order that I was a dismal failure as a writer—except when I was writing about children or animals, the powerless and dependent.

By acting on John's phone call, the direction of my college career changed and for the next few years I plugged along, finally graduating in 1985 with a degree in biology and English, i.e., creative writing. By then, with the encouragement of Evelyn Wilde Mayerson and Lester Goran, and a pat or two on the head by Isaac Bashevis Singer and James Michener, I was actually working on a novel, which eventually became *Dolphin Sky* (Putnam, 1996).

In 1988, I was still a year and a half away from finishing my flying career and getting ready to enter graduate school at Florida International University in their brand-new creative writing program.

On January 4, 1988, I was on a layover in Houston, Texas, and picked up the morning paper. In it was an article about Jane Goodall, who has dedicated her life to studying and protecting wild chimpanzees. On the same page was another story by the same feature writer, Bob Tutt. It was about Lucy, a chimpanzee raised as if she were a human child—a story that has haunted me ever since.

Lucy is the real-life Sukari. What happens to Sukari happened to Lucy. So, although this is a work of fiction, little of it is untrue. All the chimpanzees that you see as cute babies in commercials, or in movies, or in circus acts end up grown and unwanted. If they were raised as Lucy was, loved and cared for, eating her meals at the same table as her "owners," then the tragedy of being unwanted is compounded, more so because Lucy used sign language. She could communicate her feelings, her love, and her pain.

The kindest thing we can do for chimpanzees is to protect them in the wild, stop using them in senseless commercials and stupid movies, and stop locking them in small cages to use as hairy test tubes. Our DNA is 98.4 percent identical to that of chimpanzees. You can help by supporting the people who are working to protect our closest relatives.

Jane Goodall Institute

Center for Captive Chimpanzee Care
(where the Coulston Foundation chimps ended up)

The Center for Great Apes

Friends of Washoe

The International Primate League

Or check the Internet for a sanctuary for chimpanzees near you.

The American Sign Language Alphabet

a

b

c

d

i

j

k

l

m

r

s

t

u

0

1

2

3

4